The Matchmaking Fund

Christina Clare

Copyright © 2025 by Christina Clare/This and That Publishing, LLC

All rights reserved.

No part of this publication may be reproduced, distributed, stored, or transmitted in any form or by any means, including photocopying, recording, or other electronic or mechanical methods, without the prior written permission of the publisher, except as permitted by U.S. copyright law. For permission requests, contact:
This and That Publishing, LLC at thisandthatpublishing@gmail.com

The story, all names, characters, and incidents portrayed in this production are fictitious. No identification with actual persons (living or deceased), buildings, and products is intended or should be inferred.

Book Cover by Labyrinth Book Designs

First edition 2025

e-book ISBN 979-8-9903502-4-3

paperback ISBN 979-8-9903502-5-0

Printed and bound by Amazon.com Inc's Kindle Direct Publishing

<u>Austen Saints</u>

Emma St. George—chief superintendent
Jane St. George—Emma's younger sister
Anne St. James—mayor
Maryanne St. James—Anne's younger sister
Catherine St. John—Fire chief

<u>Police Officers</u>

Oliver Barnes—police constable
Nancy Halliwell—police constable
N. Bakshi—police constable
Fanny Fletcher—detective sergeant
Neville Sinclair—detective inspector

<u>Ravenswick ~~Busybodies~~ Godmothers</u>

Mrs. McCarthy—parish secretary
Charlie Lansberry—desk sergeant
Harriet "Harry" Blackthorne– secretary to Anne St. James, the mayor
Dani—desk sergeant and secretary to Emma St. George, the chief superintendent

Chapter 1

For the first time in a week, Oliver felt like he could relax at work. It had been seven days of tripping, knocking, face-planting or some other means of embarrassing himself.

The cause for such embarrassment? Their new chief superintendent in for a week-long observation of their station. Over the past seven days, his eagerness to see the beautiful brunette had morphed into sheer terror as he managed to find new ways of embarrassing himself in front of her. And once, in front of the detective sergeant, too, when he brought them both down in the hallway.

He'd never had an awkward moment in his life till the universe put him in Emma's path. He seemed to be making up for it now.

"Earth to Ollie."

Oliver looked up to find the desk sergeant Charlie Lansberry in front of him and he jumped to his feet. "Sorry, ma'am."

"No need to explain—we all know what that face means." Charlie, who was at least Oliver's mother's age, laughed and handed him a slip of paper. "Call came in about a theft at St. Margaret Ward's." It was the only Catholic parish in the surrounding area, on the edge of Ravenswick bordering the village to the east, Littleton.

Oliver took the paper and, with a wave, grabbed his hat and headed out.

"Should someone clue him in that that's the chief super's church?" the detective sergeant, Fanny Fletcher, wondered aloud.

"Where would the fun be in that?" Charlie laughed.

Emma turned her car off and just sat, staring at the back of her building, wondering how six months ago she convinced her superiors to promote her.

"Not incapable, just a little overwhelmed," Emma muttered to herself.

The building was a set of four row houses in the heart of the village, on a street lined with shops and apartments, along with the village's one café. The front of the building painted a pretty picture of a typical English village, but she hardly ever saw it since they used the back to get in and out. Her flat was the last one at the end of the road, nestled next to a wooded area. The residents of the row homes parked in the back alley that came to a dead end, with a bar blocking car access to the trees. Right now she was looking at her back door with the little enclosed garden. On the rare occasion that she was home, she could look out onto the main street and (enviously) watch people walk their dogs to the woods, or (not enviously) go for a run in the mornings and evenings.

The flat next to her was occupied by her best and oldest friend, and Ravenswick's mayor, Anne St. James. It looked like the lights were on, and Emma debated going next door, mostly for the company.

She'd never thought she would move back to the village, especially since only her younger sister, Jane, lived here. Their parents had moved to the big city the second Jane was a legal adult and was settled, sharing the third flat with Anne's baby sister, Maryanne, since they were both enrolled in the local college while Emma was off to police college.

The final townhouse apartment was occupied by the fire captain, Catherine St. John. The fact she was a year younger than Emma and Anne didn't matter; they were all lumped together in school in any extracurriculars, so they had been friends since high school when Catherine's family had moved from two towns over.

Deciding she wasn't good company, Emma grabbed her bag and locked her car. She opened the back gate and took just a moment to enjoy her tiny garden, promising herself, again, to actually do something back here. A little table, some flowers, something, so on days like today, when she questioned her sanity and cursed her ambition, she could come out with a glass of wine and just enjoy everything.

She let herself in and dropped her bag and keys on the cupboard in the entranceway. Kicking off her shoes, she debated what to do for dinner and was about to look up takeaways when there was a knock on her back door.

"I was hoping you were in and settled, but not so comfy I would be intruding," Anne called from the door.

Emma waved her in. "Mission achieved, then. Want to get some takeaways, Madam Mayor?"

"That good of a day, huh? Let's have some wine," Anne said and, knowing her way around Emma's flat, pulled out two glasses. "I need to pick your brain about something, anyway."

"Okay," Emma drawled as she watched Anne pull out a bottle of wine she brought and pour them each a glass. "What is this about?"

"First, you okay?" Because they had been friends forever, Emma knew the question was sincere.

"Just one of those days. One where I question what the hell am I doing and why the hell they picked me for this promotion."

She handed Emma one of the glasses. "Well, I can answer the last. It's because you kick ass and are amazing at your job," Anne said and clinked their glasses. "Two kick-ass women—West

England, beware. Besides, you can't become the sheriff of the county without moving up the chain."

"I know. It's just been a day."

"What, did PC Barnes trip over you?" Anne asked, amused.

"I see him walk into the doorframe once, and you haven't forgotten." Emma rolled her eyes.

Anne snorted into her glass. "Either you are a horrible chief super, or the station really likes him."

"What does that mean?"

"The poor kid is all asses and elbows around you. I have it on good authority he laid out detective sergeant Fanny Fletcher in the hallway. Last count I heard was…never mind." Anne smirked into her wine. "It's just adorable, is all. And apparently the station kept the gossip from reaching your ears, which is even more adorable."

"Absurd. He's like ten years younger than me."

"Eight."

"I'm old."

"Bite your tongue."

Emma glared at her. "You know what I mean."

"I know we're the same age and you just called me old."

"Hardly. He's a boy, and why are we even talking about this?" Emma asked, genuinely confused. "I'm hardly interested in dating anyone at the moment, let alone a cop." Not that she had ever dated. She was driven—scarily so, according to her sister Jane. At least that was what she was always told as to why boys didn't ask her out growing up.

Now she was too busy.

"What did you want?" Emma asked, changing the subject.

"Okay, I had an idea. Covid really hit this village. We rallied, but the economy is still recovering from it and then we have new challenges in this economy. It's hard for us small villages to keep going with these continuous lumps the universe is throwing at us. I have been trying to think of something to help the economy and maybe boost tourism," Anne said.

She barely took a breath, as if hoping if she went through it quickly, Emma wouldn't have space to object. "Now with Easter over and summer approaching, a small village in West England isn't going to exactly attract tourists. So I thought of an event that would raise money and highlight the local restaurants: Blind Date in Ravenswick. The name is awful, we're tabling that for now. There's only so many slots, so we can make sure everyone is paired off—ten men and ten women, specifically. I have Harry in charge of signups so everyone will know for sure that their date is single and relatively free of town gossip."

Harriet "Harry" Blackthorne had been secretary to the mayor of Ravenswick for nearly forty years. Mayors came and went; Harry did not. If village grandmother was a position, it would be Harry. Nothing happened in Ravenswick or the surrounding area that Harry and her cohort of friends didn't know of immediately.

Some who felt daring would call them gossips or busybodies. Emma appreciated living her life without looking over her shoulder. Two of Harry's friends worked in the police force, including her own secretary, Dani.

"I mean, I can see what you are trying for," Emma decided, taking a sip. "I'm assuming you'd do like a social media blast or something."

"Of course. Advertising about the event, a live drawing online as we match up people—drawing names out of a hat, basically. I haven't decided if we would just have the couple make posts or have someone take photos."

"Talk about third wheel."

"And to entice people to join, I thought I would have a few pillars of the community. People that would get others excited to join and hopefully win a date. Three men, three women whom people would think being paired with would be fun. And *who* do you know that *just* moved back?" Anne smiled widely.

Like a shark.

"No."

"Let me get you some more wine."

"Definitely not." Emma jerked her glass back. "And no. I like the idea but no thank you."

"You can't say you like the idea then back out."

"When you are putting me out there to be an enticement, I absolutely can. Not to mention I'd be about as enticing as a cold fish."

"You're beautiful, you're in a position of authority, anyone would be lucky to win a date with you." Anne shook her head. "I have three men and two women so far. I need one more woman to balance, I even got Catherine to agree to it."

"How?"

"She thought it sounded like great fun."

Sadly, Emma could see her saying that.

"One condition. You said it's for the village and charity, yes?" Emma waited for Anne to nod. "You have to do it."

"What? No. I can't! Then the numbers are uneven again and I'd have to find another male pillar in the community, then that's hardly any space left for a regular Raven," she insisted, falling back to what kids have been calling someone from Ravenswick for decades. "Besides I'm hosting it."

"Uh-huh. You want me to do it, you do it."

"Then I'm taking one of the slots slated for an important villager, and I can't justify that. I'd rather just tell Catherine you said no because you're too chicken."

"Harry will figure something out, but you are doing something too."

Anne sat back to think, absently tapping the base of her glass. "I'll see what Harry comes up with," she agreed. "But if she can't think of something that works for this, then I'm out but you are still in, deal?"

"Deal." The only way Harry wouldn't be able to figure out a way to work the Mayor into a fundraising PR event was if she was dead and buried for a week.

Suddenly both of them received a text at the same time. Emma assumed it was the group chat with the girls since they both got the text.

She was very wrong.

"Holy shit," Anne said in shock as she jumped to her feet, rereading the text while Emma went to grab her keys.

Chapter 2

Anne exited the car as Emma turned off the ignition and took in the scene in front of her. One cop car, yellow tape, and a community support officer with Mrs. McCarthy, the parish secretary, who clearly heard their arrival as she turned quickly in their direction.

As Emma got out of her car, Anne was already approaching the older woman who was nervously clasping her hands. "Mrs. McCarthy," Anne said kindly. "Is everyone all right?"

"Yes, yes, no one was here. I went in to grab some things for the morning Mass and noticed the monstrance was missing. As I was telling the constable, while it is decorative since it holds the consecrated host I can't imagine why anyone would steal it. You girls are wonderful for coming right over."

She'd known they would do exactly that when she'd texted both of them. The fact that the mayor and chief super both attended St. Margaret's, in Mrs. McCarthy's mind, meant they needed to be involved in every step of the way.

"Do you want a cup of tea? I can go in and make us both one," Anne offered.

"I'll wait for Father Michael. He is still talking with the police constable. That young Oliver."

"He's an excellent officer, Mrs. McCarthy," Emma promised.

"I never said otherwise, did I!" Mrs. McCarthy said, horrified. "Just so young. Then again, at my age, everyone is. Will you see how much longer they will be?"

Emma waved over the community support officer to sit with her.

"I love her, but to act surprised we came over when she texted the chief super and the mayor? What did she think we'd do?" Anne rolled her eyes. She gave a gentle elbow bump as they approached the door. "Young Oliver is here," she teased.

"And?"

"You are *not* that dense." Anne laughed. "That boy is half in love with you."

"First, you just called him a boy, and Mrs. McCarthy made it a point to point out he's young," Emma rolled her eyes. "Second, it's a schoolboy crush. Cute, harmless, and easily moved on from."

"Except we're not in school," Anne lowered her voice since they entered the church. "And younger, yes, but he is most definitely a man."

Emma shot her a look but couldn't snap back as they approached the transept, where Father Michael was talking to PC Oliver Barnes. He was facing the door and noticed their entrance, offering a small head nod as they approached.

"I apologize for Mrs. McCarthy bothering you both," Father Michael said. "It is good of both of you to come."

Oliver turned and dropped his notebook, catching it midair.

Emma smiled. "Nice save."

"How are you, Father? Mrs. McCarthy said no one was injured?" Anne asked, genuinely concerned.

"No one. As I was telling PC Barnes, I don't know when anyone was in the room last. Only those who signed up for perpetual adoration five days ago, including yourself." Father Michael nodded towards Emma, and Oliver's face went from red to white in the blink of an eye.

"For the record, Officer Barnes, the monstrance was still on the alter when I left at 5 a.m. and Tiffany took over. Mrs. McCarthy is eager to check on you herself," Emma said. "I have every faith in my officers and trust PC Barnes will find the monstrance, Father."

"Even if that means interrogating the chief super." Anne smiled widely, a glint of mischief in her eyes that caused Father Michael to laugh as he watched Oliver blush again.

The priest said, "I'll see you both at Mass on Sunday, if not before."

When Father Michael went to join Mrs. McCarthy, Emma turned to Oliver. "Get me caught up, Barnes."

"Ma'am. Uh..." He looked to his scrawled notes, trying to focus. "Not sure on how entry was made yet—the techs are still working. Neither Father Michael nor Mrs. McCarthy saw anyone suspicious today around the church."

Anne smiled, and a lifetime of friendship told Emma to be worried. "I don't think I've actually seen anyone with hearts in their eyes before, but there's a first for everything," she gushed.

"Anne!" Emma gasped, exasperated.

"What? It's adorable. For the record, I also have faith you'll find the monstrance, Barnes." Anne grinned.

"Yes, ma'am. Thank you, Madam Mayor."

"If we don't leave, he may dehydrate from blushing." Anne laughed.

She wasn't sure what confused her more, what Anne said or what drove her to say it. "What has gotten into you?" Now Emma was blushing, too, and she wanted to throttle her friend. Instead she pushed her down the aisle before turning back to Oliver. "I'm sorry about that, Barnes. I can only say she's either intoxicated or an idiot."

"Yes ma'am."

"Did you just call my friend and mayor a drunk idiot?" Emma asked.

"What? No!"

Emma smiled. "Relax, Barnes. I know you wouldn't. You know, I could have been your babysitter when you were growing up."

"It's not too late." The way his eyes widened to the size of saucers made her smile.

Warm chocolate brown, she realized; *Dear Lord they're pretty*, she thought, then shook her head. Anne was putting these ideas into her head, and she was clearly sleep-deprived or something. It was the only thing she could think of.

"Oh shit," Oliver said. "Sorry ma'am. It's the end of a long shift I don't know what I'm saying anymore."

She didn't know what she was thinking, either. "Tell you what—you focus on finding the monstrance, and we'll both forget everything else that happened tonight." Emma turned on her heel.

Anne was waiting at the entrance, and Emma practically pushed her out to the car. "What the hell was that?"

"I feel a teensy bit guilty about teasing him, but I couldn't help it."

"One glass of wine and you have no self-control?" Emma demanded.

When they were both in the car, Anne turned to study her as she clicked her seat belt. "Why are you worked up over it? I didn't embarrass you."

"He's my officer, one of the good ones, Anne. How can he do his work if he's being poked and prodded by your acerbic tongue?"

"Hmm, well, I'm pretty sure he wants to do the poking and prodding to you," Anne teased as Emma backed out.

Emma slammed the brakes as she turned to straighten the car, both of them jerking with the movement. "Anne!"

"And now you're blushing," Anne laughed. "Lord, I'm covering your entrance fee for the event, because tonight was so damn entertaining."

There was a beat before Emma snapped out, "Entrance fee? You wanted me to *pay,* too?"

"Not anymore." Anne smirked as they turned down the lane that led to the back of their building. "Covers the meals, with what's left over going to local charities. Probably food pantry, as that's on theme."

Emma took a deep breath as she parked in her spot. She gave her a look as she undid her belt. "Remember, you have to do it too."

"Only if Harry can think of a way," Anne said. They just sat there a moment. It was the perk of being neighbors; Emma was just on the other side of the garden wall. "I do appreciate you doing this," Anne said sincerely.

"You caught me in a good mood. Good thing you asked before all that in the church." Emma opened the door and got out.

"See you later," Anne called out as she studied her friend walking into her portion of the garden, then inside.

It was nearing the end of the workday the following day when Emma's cell rang. She half expected it to be Mrs. McCarthy fishing for an update—which made her think of Oliver and the night prior.

Anne, thankfully. "Everything okay?" She was curious about what couldn't wait till they both got home that night.

"You'll be happy to know Harry has what she's calling the 'perfect' idea for this, and I hate you."

Emma laughed. "Whatever it is I'm sure I am going to love it." She waved off the secretary outside her door about to enter. She could give Anne two minutes to hear this.

"Sure, you're not the one being raffled like a prize heifer," Anne huffed. "Harry swears it will bring in crazy donations for the charity event. A blind auction to win a date with the mayor. Lord, it's going to be so embarrassing. What if no one bids?"

"I promise I'll bid, just to make sure there's one."

"What if I only bring in like twenty pounds?" Anne worried aloud. "Why did I agree to do this?"

"It's going to be great, and you'll bring in a ton of money," Emma promised. "Have you decided on a charity? Or a name?"

"Not yet. There's only two charities in the village. If we expand to the county, there's more. I'm thinking the food pantry still—I don't think we'll have enough to split between our two. Bloody hell, now I'm going to stress over this. I put Harry in charge of it, with the help of the intern on the tech stuff, and told her not to tell me how much the auction goes for. She'll tell you and then you can tell me if I need to be embarrassed."

"It's a blind auction, No one has to know."

"The winner will know," Anne pointed out. "Gotta go. I hate you."

Anne hung up as the fire chief walked in. "Catherine, what can I do for you?"

Anne thought of Catherine—who stood at least five foot ten, with dark hair and dark eyes—as their local Amazon warrior fighting fires and saving the day.

"Dropping off my entrance fee or whatever it's called," she said and dropped an envelope on her desk.

"Wait," Anne said and grabbed the envelope taking a peak inside. "It's fifty pounds," she reminded her. "This is...why is there an extra fifty in here?"

"Funny you should mention that."

"I don't take bribes. What do you take me for? Seriously, after all these years? Besides, it's a dinner date at a local restaurant," Anne pointed out. "Not exactly something I'd think worth a fifty-pound bribe."

"Think of it as a donation for the charity," Catherine said unbothered. "And it's not for me."

Anne leaned back in her chair. Now that her shock was over, her bluster was gone. She studied her friend. "Now I'm really confused."

"Rumor has it Oliver also signed up."

"Yeah, his sister dragged him in this morning before work," Anne nodded. "He was the tenth guy to sign up, so we are good on the males."

"And Emma signed up."

"Yes," Anne said slowly.

"Think of it as a donation to get the two of them paired up in this." Catherine grinned.

"No." Anne stared at her in shock. "Really?"

"It will be worth it, I fully plan on walking by or eating out at the restaurant during their date. But the kid is so lovesick, it's adorable." Catherine smiled. "I think of it as giving fate a helping hand."

"Fate is very busy, after all." Anne smirked as she put the envelope in her desk drawer. "Wait, joking aside, why are you interested?"

"We're all pretty much the same age, and if I had a younger man look at me the way Oliver looks at Emma, I'd want someone to give me the nudge." Catherine shrugged. "Just imagine the fun with a little fling."

"Now I'm jealous," Anne sighed. "But I fully agree. Do you work Friday night?"

"Not this week."

"We should all get together and do something," Anne decided. "I'll send a group text."

"Sounds good." Catherine waved as she left.

Harry entered. "Here."

"What's this?"

"Another contribution to the Emma and Oliver fund."

"Wait, what?"

"Have you ever known Emma to take time for herself? For fun?" Harry rested one hand on her hip, finger tapping. "She's the most driven girl I've ever seen in my life. And she's achieved a lot—don't get me wrong. But all the more reason for that girl to have some fun."

Anne smiled and added the envelope to her drawer. "Now I just have to find a way to rig a live draw matching couples on social media."

"If you can't figure out how to fake a live event, what kind of politician are you?" Harry drawled, making her laugh. Then Harry studied the mayor. "You gave in to all that surprisingly fast."

"I don't see it as a real bribe. I don't receive anything from it, and neither does Catherine. The money goes to charity." Anne shrugged dismissively. Whether Harry believed her or not wasn't clear, but she left Anne to her work.

It was partially true. That extra seventy-five pounds from Catherine and Harry would go to charity. At least it wouldn't be an insubstantial sum.

The reality was, though, she hadn't stopped thinking about the previous night. She hadn't commented on it, but the fact was that Emma had blushed and had gotten very defensive of Oliver. All of which Anne found interesting. She had no doubt Oliver would be a great date, if he relaxed in Emma's presence, and she wanted to give Emma that because she knew her friend had given up. So if she could rig this to give Emma one special moment with someone who adored her, as a confidence boost, she would.

What Anne forgot was it was Ravenswick. Perk or curse, small town life meant everyone knew everyone and everything. Which meant Oliver's crush on Emma was known by all. Word spread as it always did, and by the end of the week the *Emma and Oliver Matchmaking Fund*, as people were calling it, had nearly four hundred pounds in donations.

"Holy shit," Anne said looking at the final tally before they launched the online auction for her. "If I don't bring in half that I am going to be depressed. Does anyone even have money left? When this ends horribly all of you are fired."

Harry smirked. "Sure. Meanwhile, you could make saint status for this matchmaking endeavor."

Ravenswick's first annual Matchmaking Madness, Anne thought. She turned to Harry and her intern. "All right, here we go. Now, let's practice how to rig this drawing live on social media."

Chapter 3

Emma opened the social media website up on her office computer. She normally didn't use office equipment for personal use, but she chalked it up to community relations, since it wasn't outright banned.

"Welcome, everyone, and I hope you're having a wonderful Friday afternoon!" Anne's chipper voice came across as Emma grabbed some files she needed to go through. She didn't even know who all the men were—although everyone seemed to make sure she knew Oliver was the last to join for the men. All the girls, several of her staff, random people she bumped into around the village.

"With all of your help, we have twenty people who are waiting to find out who their blind date will be with! Here's a quick reminder of how this works." Anne pointed to the small wheel cage on her desk. "We could only find one of these, so we put the numbers for our ladies here. It's the order of signups—you can see what number you are in our pinned post." Anne smiled. "We'll draw the woman's number, and then I'll draw the number for the man out of this purse—thanks, Harry—and we will have a pair! Harry will pick one of our local restaurants for the couple's date. Remember, two couples will have breakfast dates at our local café and bakery. And thanks to some generous donors, we have raised additional money for our local charity. I'll announce the final total at the end," Anne promised.

She twirled the contraption with the women's numbers. "Our first lady is number eight," she read.

"Vera Stephrem," Harry checked the sheet.

"And Vera, your date will be with number four," Anne pulled out.

Three more couples were drawn, and then Emma stopped when she heard her name. "And Emma's date will be number ten," Anne announced.

"Oliver Barnes," Harry said, and Emma felt her face.

"What the *hell*?" She put a hand up to touch her cheek and swore she could feel it burning.

"At *Farina e Fiori*," Harry added, and Emma just leaned back in her chair.

She was going on a date to the Italian restaurant, arguably Ravenswick's best restaurant, with the boy who had a crush on her. And she couldn't even call Anne to yell at her because she was still drawing couples.

Her phone rang and she saw it was her sister, Jane. She picked up.

"What the hell? I mean, *there were ten options.*"

"I know! It's so adorable," Jane gushed. "And the Italian restaurant! I was worried you'd get the café, which is wonderful, but a breakfast date just seems wrong for a first date."

"Jaaane." She drew out her sister's name so it was three syllables long. "I can't do this," she hissed.

"Uh, it's a little late?" Jane pointed out. "Three hundred people watched it on live, and it will be on social media forever."

"Three hundred? What, did the whole bloody village watch?"

"You want people to think you were too chicken to go out on a blind date? Especially a blind date that wasn't even a blind date?"

"Jane. I'm his boss."

"Technically you're, like, his boss's boss's boss, right?" Jane tried to think. "It's for a good cause. It's not like it's a real date. And hey, didn't Anne pay for your entrance fee? You're not even out any money."

"Stop being rational."

Jane laughed. "When did you turn into such a grump? While I have you on the phone, I'm assuming you booked our flights for next month. You never told me how much I owe you."

"They are, and I'll have to double check later."

"The important question is, can the two of you talk about something besides work?" Jane wondered aloud. "I can't remember your last date. It had to have been when you were in London."

"Oh my God," Jane's gasp had Emma sitting up straight. "Did you see who Anne's date is with?"

"I stopped paying attention because, you know, *Oliver*. Who?"

"David Stratham."

"Oh. My. God." Lord Stratham, the local county noble? "How much do you think he paid?"

"Obviously more than anyone else," Jane drawled.

"Harry's suppose to tell me. And I'll hold out on telling Anne just because."

"But you'll tell me, right?"

"Of course. How am I supposed to look anyone here in the face?" Emma demanded, feeling like they were all staring at her.

The quick head snaps at the desks she could see outside her office when she looked up certainly confirmed that feeling.

"What can anyone say? It was luck of the draw," Jane consoled her. "If anything, they are probably saying Oliver's dream is coming true. Poor boy's probably beside himself." Jane snorted.

"For wanting me to not stress over this, people really need to stop referring to him as *boy*," Emma snapped. "I have to go to work." She hit the button to disconnect and turned around in her chair to face out the window.

One meal. That was all. She could handle that. It was for a good cause. *Please God.*

Fanny watched Oliver and his partner, Nancy, head out on something related to the St. Margaret burglary. "I don't think I've seen anyone's color—sir?" she asked, jumping up as the inspector went running over to Oliver's desk.

Tall and lanky, with a laid-back attitude, the inspector was not known for taking decisive action like this, hurling himself towards the desk. "Have to get here before the screen times out!"

"Sir?"

A couple clicks with the mouse. "There." Neville smiled, clearly pleased with himself like a child conquering the playground. "Let's grab a coffee, Sergeant."

"Really? You think that is going to keep me out of the loop?" Charlie looked amused. "Bring me back one of those tea lattes," she told them.

"Do I want to know?" Fanny sighed as she followed him out.

"If you want to plead ignorance, then now is the time to say so," Neville said easily.

"Hell no."

"Oliver left without signing out of the computer. He also never signs out of his social media on his computer."

Fanny nodded. They were all guilty of that at times. As long as you signed out of the computer, no one else could easily get to your signed-in sites, as it required each individual's ID card to sign in. They were a small station—all of fifteen people—but they had modern computing.

"So I sent a friend request from Oliver to Emma." He looked smug as they reached the café and he held the door open for her.

"No!" Fanny laughed. "He was already borderline faint when he saw he 'won' the draw with the chief super. This may give him a heart attack."

"I think Oliver will surprise everyone, especially the chief super," Neville smiled as Fanny placed their coffee order, including Charlie's latte.

"He looks fine." Oliver could hear his roommate in his room while he waited on Oliver to change in the bathroom.

"Almost passable. What about this?" His sister suggested holding up a shirt as he walked in. Both decided to provide their opinions on his date attire.

"I can't believe I am saying this, but I almost wish it was over with." Oliver jerked the shirt out of his sister's hands. Between Victoria, his well-intentioned-yet-busybody sister, and James, his laid-back, devil-may-care roommate and best friend, it was like a game of tennis with their suggestions. "God, who sent the friend request? Why did she accept?"

"You'd rather she didn't accept?" James pointed out.

"Just be yourself, but not, like, *so* yourself," Victoria repeated for the third time the past week. "You don't want to remind her of your age."

"It's amazing he didn't forget that in the twenty-four minutes since you last told him," James rolled his eyes.

"Thank God she's not seeing the travesty that is your apartment." Victoria rolled her eyes **back at him.**

"Focus. I don't need to worry over what else is potentially embarrassing," Oliver snapped as he buttoned up the third shirt. "Okay, no more. No more suggestions, wardrobe changes, sniping at each other."

"You wouldn't know he has a high-stress job," James said in a faux aside to Victoria.

"No where near as stressful as hers, I'm sure," she said.

"You know, not everything is a competition," Oliver pointed out as he grabbed his wallet.

"Sure," they said in tandem, laughing.

He wasn't sure what would be worse: the stress in the leadup to his date with Emma—*saints be praised*—or having to relive it with these two afterwards. And his partner tomorrow.

"Look, the odds were one in ten," his sister finally said, her tone serious yet soft for the first time since she burst into his apartment. "And let's be honest—if the fates hadn't intervened, the odds would have been zero, because you would never have asked her out on your own."

James rolled his eyes. "One hell of a pep talk, Vicki."

"All I am saying is, this is your chance. Take it. Show her what an amazing guy you are. I'm sure she has her own worries over tonight, so be yourself. You can be charming when you want to be. I'm not saying she's going to fall madly in love with you," she added quickly, "but you can at least show her you have something to offer and she should take you seriously. Especially after all the snafus at work."

"Maybe don't remind her of those," James added.

Oliver shot him a dirty look. Like hell he'd remind her of the most embarrassing week of his life.

"You got this!" Victoria encouraged him as he walked out, sharing a look with James.

"Ten says he dumps an entrée on her," James offered Victoria his hand.

She shook it, grinning. "You're on."

Chapter 4

Like every drive in Ravenswick, it seemed, the drive from Emma's flat to the restaurant was approximately five minutes with no traffic. She got there early and sat in her car. After checking her makeup for the third time in as many minutes, she saw Oliver arrive and took a deep breath.

It's a date, Emma. It's a meal, some conversation, then home. She'd endured more terrifying things in her career, like the interview that had gotten her this job. Right? She would enjoy the free food and hope no horrible photos ended up online. *Please God—that is the last thing I need.* She had barely started this new role, and while she couldn't see how this date would derail everything, she was also waiting for the other shoe to drop.

Not giving herself time to think about it, she opened her door and smiled when Oliver saw her. No mistaking the way his face lit up, and that was a boost to her ego.

"Hiya. Thanks for agreeing to meet here," Emma said as Oliver opened the door to the restaurant for her.

"Of course. I—"

He was interrupted as what looked like the entire staff of *Farina e Fiori* gathered around them.

"Welcome!" one of them, a well-dressed man, said. "Welcome to *Farina e Fiori*! Please, allow me to show you to your seats."

Emma was pretty sure he was the owner. He wasn't dressed in the staff's uniform, and she had seen him coming and going several times from the restaurant and handling the deposits. Emma and Oliver shared a look as they followed the man and, in turn, were followed by two of the four waitresses to a table secluded in the corner.

"I have taken the pleasure of putting together a special menu for you two," the man said. "I hope no one has any allergies?" They barely were able to nod before he bustled out. One woman placed glasses of water before them and another handed Oliver a wine menu.

"Whatever the chef thinks appropriate for this special menu," Oliver said, handing it back.

When they were finally alone, Emma leaned closer—small towns, big ears. "Do you think the other lottery couple got this level of attention?"

Oliver laughed and she saw him relax. "I'm sorry for not asking you about the wine. I thought Luigi might cry if I made a poor choice."

Emma laughed as one of the girls brought them their wine and appetizers. "I was pretty sure he's the owner."

"His father created the restaurant, using his mother's recipes. She worked in the kitchen till she was at least eighty. At least, to a young boy, that's what it looked like. Luigi prides himself on learning from his Nonna's knee."

"Then best not to contradict any of his choices," Emma agreed with a smile. "We don't need to give Anne any embarrassing photos for her social media campaign."

"Do you think she's here? I didn't see her."

"Not her personally, but she has spies. I didn't get a good look at who all was here, so I didn't see if anyone from the Mayor's office was in." Or her sister, or even Catherine. "I wouldn't put it past my own sister to agree to being her spy. The only reason I know for sure Catherine isn't is because she's on shift."

Oliver grinned, and she realized she could stare at that smile for ages. He was cute.

Tonight his coal-colored pants and a forest green button down emphasized he was tall and lanky and made his whiskey brown hair pop.

Carved by Michaelangelo but sure, 'cute,' Emma, she mentally chided herself. She never really saw Oliver before, she realized, only ever in uniform as part of a team. Well, cute was an understatement, but there was something else about him she couldn't put her finger on.

You didn't become chief super for your looks, Emma she reminded herself. She'd figure it out by the end of dinner if it killed her, but it definitely caught her attention.

"I think I may have seen the intern for the mayor's office when we got here. It looked like she was on a date; she was with another girl her age. Normally I'd think nothing of it, but..." He shrugged.

"I wouldn't put it past Anne to send an intern as a spy."

"For all the dates, or just ours?" Oliver wondered aloud, leaning back as someone came to clear their plates.

The way the low lighting and candles reflected on him, he should be advertising for the restaurant as he sat in the candlelight. "I don't know if I've seen you out of uniform before. Oh God." Emma realized what she said and slapped a hand over her mouth. "In civilian clothes!"

"That makes us even, I think," Oliver said, smiling. "At least as far as embarrassing phrases coming out of my mouth." God, if he thought about when he bumped into her at the church, he would feel his face flush. *Don't go there, Ollie.*

"What comment?" Emma asked, relieved. "I promise not to talk shop. What do you do when you're not working?"

They talked hobbies and books as their main course was served. She realized before dessert what it was about Oliver she couldn't put her finger on; it hit her halfway through the main course—he was *comfortable* with himself. She had only seen him in the context of work and knew he was a good officer and a good teammate. What she never saw before was *him*. Part of that was because of that crush of his, but she never saw him outside of work.

There was no false bravado of youth or insecurity about who he was. Nor was he full of himself, like the men ahead of her in command, and she couldn't see Oliver turning into them. He was comfortable with himself in a way she didn't see too often.

Her thoughts were interrupted by the waitress asking, "Chef would like to know if you would be interested in dessert?"

"Yes," Emma said immediately. As the waitress left, she added to Oliver, "Dessert is never a no." Ordering dessert also meant she had a little more time to settle after her revelation.

"I make it a point to never contradict my date." Oliver smiled and she found *herself* unsettled. *Think about it later, Em* she told herself. *Enjoy this, because who the bloody hell would have thought you would enjoy a date with Oliver Barnes?*

Oliver knew when a date was a disaster. He had a good sense when a lady was going to blow him off—not that it happened often. Most dates were enjoyable enough to repeat a few times, but burned out quickly.

It so far had been the best seventy minutes of his life, and he hoped they were making dessert from scratch in the kitchen, because he wanted every moment he could have with Emma. *If this is my one shot, I need every moment I can get.*

He had never wanted a date to go well so badly in his life, and he had no idea how this would end. He knew it wasn't a disaster—far, far from it. He also knew this was not going to burn out quickly; not for him, at least.

He was half-in love with Emma St. George already.

What he wasn't sure of, not completely, was her.

Dessert was one giant gelato dish with two spoons, and he could have kissed the chef, the owner, and the mayor for this.

"This looks delicious," Emma said to the waitress. "I had no idea you had gelato!"

"Mr. Tucci added it to the menu recently. One day we may have a gelato station," their waitress said. "Enjoy!"

"Don't think less of me for digging right in," Emma told Oliver. She took a bite and the flavor burst in her mouth.

He couldn't help but smile. She had enjoyed everything the chef made and it was never a secret. "Why on earth would I think less of you?" he asked, perplexed. He was making mental notes of what she liked and disliked. The first wine had been too dry to her taste, so he'd asked for something different. Otherwise, she'd enjoyed everything.

He hoped she enjoyed his company half as much as he enjoyed hers.

"I remember reading in magazines growing up about how you shouldn't order too much food on a date, and avoid certain types of food. From what I hear from Maryanne," she added, naming the mayor's sister, "the dating advice hasn't changed; just the technology. Half the time I shake my head over the same old 'advice' being spread around by teenagers. I don't know how she deals with teens every day."

"Dumb advice," Oliver said. "How is she adjusting to being back in Ravenswick? She's quieter than I remember." Maryanne had been the one to leave for college, and everyone had assumed she'd only visit for major holidays. What most didn't know was that she'd moved back after leaving an abusive relationship.

"She's quieter." Emma sighed. "We both moved back around the same time, I haven't seen her in years before that. Anne worries constantly about her. She was worried that staying with her would be stifling since she was always a protective big sister. Hopefully living with my sister, who's her best friend, and being surrounded by the rest of us helps."

"We're all keeping an eye out for that ex of hers," Oliver promised.

"I never doubted it," Emma said. She looked down and realized they had finished the last of the gelato. "I hate to end the evening on a sour note."

He managed to *not* blurt out anything embarrassing, thank God. Instead he took her hand on the top of the table in his, but didn't look away from her. "Want more dessert?"

She laughed as he hoped and didn't pull her hand away. "Don't make me break my 'never no to dessert' rule."

"Question withdrawn." He stood and pulled her chair out for her. She took a quick look around as they walked to the exit; the restaurant was much busier than when they had first arrived.

While he held the door open, he saw the same college-age girl he saw at the beginning and this time got a good look at her.

"I'm positive she is the mayor's intern," he said as he walked her to her car.

"I'm not surprised. I honestly expected Anne to send someone since she wants to do a social media campaign."

"Would it offend you if I said I could see any of the Austen Saints volunteering to spy?"

She laughed as they reached her car but didn't make a move to open her door. "Austen Saints? That's what they're calling us now?"

"All four of you living in the same building? Rumor has it your mothers were part of a Jane Austen book club and vowed to name all of you after her heroines. Then the fact all of your surnames begin with Saint. Really, we would be doing a disservice by *not* calling you that." He moved so his body shielded her from view in case anyone from the restaurant was trying to spy or take photos. "You know, there are four other restaurants in town. If we brought this much publicity for one, it only seems fair we do the same for the others."

"Oliver."

"Emma." The air practically sizzled with electricity, and he was itching to reach for her hand. "Unless you are afraid to go out with me again?"

Her eyes narrowed but she shifted closer. "That's a dirty move, constable."

"Four more dates. Admit it, you had fun tonight," he challenged.

He'd managed to relax after the initial impact of seeing her because she looked stunning exiting her car. She was only a few inches shorter than him in her shoes, which meant that when he stood next to her, he could see the gold flecks in her hazel eyes. He was pretty sure they'd haunt his dreams for the next several nights.

He'd taken his sister's advice, deciding if this was his one shot, he was going to give it his all by just being himself. He knew what he was about, at least.

At least up until this moment. What the hell was coming over him?

"Two of those are local pubs," Emma said. "Nothing against them, but everyone goes there after work. Running into your colleagues, people I am in charge of, is not my idea of a date, and I am sure they would not appreciate their boss showing up."

"We'll skip those," he said easily. "I have a morning shift on Monday. What do you say to a breakfast date then?"

She grabbed her door handle behind her and pulled it open, but never turned away from him. "Monday, then."

He leaned in to kiss her cheek and may have hovered for just a moment longer. She didn't pull away, either.

"Goodnight, Emma."

"Goodnight, Oliver."

He slipped his hands into his back pockets as he watched her get adjusted before driving away.

He just barely caught himself from doing a fist pump when he turned and realized someone in the restaurant could very easily get a photo of it.

Chapter 5

Emma wrapped up in her robe after her shower and fell onto her bed. She grabbed the pillow closest to her to pull close and closed her eyes. Sleep was the furthest thing from her mind. Even after showering, she could still feel the way Oliver's lips brushed over her cheek. She could still smell his cologne.

She was clearly smitten, and that had to be a crime.

A knock made her groan. She didn't want to get up, didn't want to move; she just wanted to bask in whatever these feelings were.

"You have one chance to get rid of us and one chance only," Jane's voice called out to her from the kitchen and Emma jumped up. She ran down the stairs to see all the Austen girls had entered her back door and were in her kitchen.

With a bottle of wine and lots of dessert. "Details now," Jane ordered as Anne grabbed glasses for everyone. Catherine was opening the wine with a pop while Maryanne pulled out the disposable plates they had brought.

"What on earth?"

"She's in her robe. Were you basking or wallowing?" Jane asked.

"What are you talking about?"

"That is your cozy outfit. You were either basking after a great date, or wallowing after a horrible one," Jane explained as Catherine poured wine.

"She's blushing." Anne grinned as she handed everyone some of the cookies and took a glass of wine her sister handed over. "Details. All the details."

"You'll see all the details. You had a spy there. It was a charity date; that's all."

"*This* does not look like charity to me," Anne said and flipped the phone around. It was a candid shot her intern had snapped during the dinner. "We all expected the hearts in Oliver's eyes. He's an anime character come to life in that regard. But girl! Look at you!"

"What, what?"

"You look gorgeous, and you also look like you're enjoying yourself." Catherine smiled into her wine. "I think the photo should be on the front page, but I was vetoed on that."

"I am going to have to confiscate your phone at this point," Emma threatened Anne. Laughing, Anne texted Emma the photo in question. She honestly wasn't going to post that one on the social media sites because it felt too personal. All joking aside, none of them had any doubts the charity date had turned into a real one.

"I'm so jealous." Maryanne sighed. "I knew I should have signed up for this."

"Next time. There wasn't anyone good enough for my baby sister," Anne said.

Jane turned back to her sister. "You look like you are enjoying yourself."

"The food was amazing. The owner, Luigi, served us himself and put together a menu for the evening. I'm curious if he picks different food for the other couple that got the restaurant." Emma decided more dessert was proper and took a bite of the cookie as the other girls groaned.

"You can't do that to us. You're not that dense. Dear Lord, she's not that dense." Catherine shook her head.

"Did Oliver trip over anything?" Maryanne asked. "No entrée ended up in your lap?"

"No. Again, he does something once. Give him a break."

The other girls shared a look and, despite some giggling, no one corrected her. "Come on, give us a play-by-play."

"There's nothing to share. The food was amazing. The wine was amazing. Despite the mayoral paparazzi, the night was ...fun." She tested how the word sounded aloud and decided it felt right.

"And? That's *it*?" Jane demanded.

"He walked me across the street to my car. Even though I am the chief super and more than capable of walking myself."

"Still sweet," Maryanne decided.

"Don't tell me you called him Constable or Barnes all evening," Jane said worriedly.

"No, I called him Oliver. He called me Emma." Emma smiled. Not even the giddy looks the girls shared soured her mood. "He kissed my cheek. God, his cologne is divine," she admitted, and the cacophony of giggling continued.

"Well, that's sweet, I suppose." Catherine sighed. "I'll admit, I was kind of hoping Oliver would, I don't know, do something. I don't mean *do* something, but I guess be a little braver."

"You mean like ask me out again?"

Every pair of eyes turned to her. "He did?" Maryanne gushed. "He asked you out on another date?"

"No."

The disappointment was palpable. She grinned into her wine glass. "He asked me out on four."

The squeals had to be audible from outside, making her laugh.

Anne gently wacked her with a pillow from the couch. "You minx!"

"Details!" Jane demanded.

Emma set her glass down and cuddled the pillow. "He asked me to go out with him again, to the other restaurants in town. I said no."

"You are giving me heart palpitations," Catherine declared.

Emma laughed as she leaned forward into the pillow. "I told him two were pubs, and we would end up being there the same time others went off shift—and no one wants to drink with the chief super."

"Oliver clearly does." Maryanne smirked. This time Emma wacked her with the pillow.

"Okay, so wait, that leaves two. The café and the Chinese restaurant," Anne said.

"Yes."

"That's so cute!" Jane squealed and plopped herself on the couch next to her to give her a hug. "I wasn't sure if he would have the balls to ask you out properly."

"You were so sure I'd say yes if he did?"

"No, but I knew you wouldn't ask him out, so he would have to find his courage. When are you going out again? Where?" Jane asked.

"Monday breakfast date. Kiss on the cheek, then I came home."

Jane sighed as she leaned against her. The other girls, while spread out in her living room all wore matching satisfied smiles.

"No photos on these, though," Emma warned her. "No spying, either," she added to all the girls.

"I can live with that, since I'm living vicariously through you. Here's to wine-and-chocolate date recaps, then," Catherine decided. "My date is with Spencer, so the best we can hope for is the free food."

"Here's to Oliver, finding his courage then," Anne said and gestured with her glass. Emma rolled her eyes as the others toasted and cheered him on.

Monday was still several days away. Five, to be precise. Ollie dealt with the good-natured ribbing from his colleagues because he was just *happy*. No disaster on the village's social media or perpetual gossip. He even had a second date coming up—a fact he kept to himself for the moment.

"What I still don't know is which of you sent Emma the friend request," Oliver told his partner, Nancy, as they reached the patrol car. As it was her turn to drive, he eased himself into the passenger seat.

"How could it have been me? We're practically attached at the hip while on duty," Nancy pointed out.

"You're the one person I do trust."

Nancy laughed as she signaled to turn down a street. They were heading to the main drag, where they had a few more doorbell cameras and neighborhood cams to collect and review, hopefully one of them caught whoever stole the monstrance. "You are sounding like a conspiracy theorist there for a second, mate. Why would anyone be out to get you? Besides, didn't it work out?"

"In that she accepted? Yeah. In that I looked like a desperate young fool? Also yeah."

Nancy shook her head. "I doubt the person did it to make you look desperate," she assured him and pulled in front of the first house on their list. "Honestly, though, the date went well, yeah?"

There was no subtlety in Oliver's grin; the joy and excitement from the date clearly evidenced. "Yeah. You can keep quiet, right?"

"Hey, what happens in the patrol car stays between us."

"We're getting breakfast in a few days, a breakfast date." He grinned.

Nancy's mouth formed an O in shock. "Get out of here! Seriously! That's great, Ollie! Wow, you really pulled it together last night."

"Hey!" he said opening his door and she followed suit. "Did you doubt me?"

"I saw the way you collied with DS Fletcher, remember? I thought for sure you broke one of her ribs."

"All right, fair. I was worried too. Thank God Emma didn't see that."

Nancy laughed as they approached the door and knocked. It took an hour to collect the missing footage from people who never emailed it in.

Oliver sighed as they pulled back to the police station. "What are the odds we find the thief on these and get the monstrance back soon? Before our next date?"

"Sadly, slim to none. We have several hours to go through on these," Nancy pointed out.

Oliver nodded and grabbed the drives they had collected. They were running out of options. So far no other cameras had caught anything suspicious on the day of the burglary. Two streets remained and if they didn't have anything they would have to pivot.

The fact they both lived in the same village meant Oliver was guaranteed to see Emma every day. What he hadn't counted on was taking a seat next to his sister in the pew on Sunday and seeing Emma, in her dress uniform with pip and crown on display on her shoulder, sitting next to Anne St. James.

"Bloody hell?" Victoria whispered in shock when she saw them a moment after him. "But she's Catholic! They both are."

The Reverend Paul Smith, despite easily being in his seventies and frail as moth wings, commanded attention when he motioned for everyone to be seated as the opening hymn finished.

Oliver had almost skipped service today, and now he wouldn't be able to pay attention to Reverend Paul at all. Judging by the looks the other congregants were giving him and Emma, it seemed no one was paying attention to Reverend Paul.

"Now, I am sure several of you recognize we have two new, familiar faces. Don't act like I can't see you down there," he told the congregants. "Mayor St. James and Chief-Superintendent St. George have joined us today to worship as we continue into this Easter season. While I know they are always happy to hear from us the people, let's keep it polite and appropriate for the Lord's Day, yes?" Reverend Paul said, with a harsh glare at a particular section of the church. Most, including Emma and Anne, chuckled as the Reverend switched to prayers.

When service finally ended at sixty-two minutes after the opening hymn—not that Oliver was keeping track—he tried to see what Emma was doing. She was sitting at the front, which put practically as much distance as possible between them inside the church.

"I don't think she's made it out yet," Victoria said softly so the nosy parkers around them couldn't hear them. She matched his slowing pace, letting others push past them to shake the Reverend's hand outside.

Suddenly Anne was in front of him and blocking his view. "Ah, Officer Barnes. And I think you are his sister."

"Mayor St. James." Oliver stood straighter. "Yes, this is Victoria," he added quickly.

"Nice to meet you in person, ma'am!" Victoria said with an impish grin. "Can I say, the blind date event was *inspired*. I'm so glad I convinced Ollie to go through with it."

Anne laughed. "That makes two of us. You'll have to sign up when we do it again."

"She will," Oliver promised with a look that promised retribution.

Completely unthreatened and unbothered—Victoria had grown up with that look, after all—she shrugged. "It will depend on what men sign up." That made Anne laugh again.

"I'm off to thank the reverend. Barnes, don't forget she's here working," Anne added before turning to leave.

Victoria shook her head. "And just like that. Rude."

"Not rude, a reminder," Oliver tried to explain as he and Victoria left. He realized they had no reason to be hanging around at the back of the church now that they weren't talking with the mayor and would draw attention to themselves—and by extension, to Emma, since she was the reason he was lingering.

"That makes no sense," Victoria said as he ushered her out.

He couldn't *not* say anything to her, though. He knew the other congregants were watching, and word would spread around Ravenswick. No matter what he did, word would spread.

Look at that Ollie Barnes pining after the chief super.
Look at the audacity of that Barnes Boy.

He didn't mind for himself, but he worried any gossip would spread its way up the police ladder. It couldn't hurt him—he was just a constable and had no plans to move upward. When Emma left the village everyone knew it was to go conquer the world, and this was just the latest stop on that journey.

"Chief super," Oliver smiled at her. Was he imagining the relief in her eyes?

"Barnes. Hello," she turned to Victoria and offered her hand. "I don't believe we've met."

"No but I feel like I already know you," Victoria said with a smile, and Oliver wanted to shake her. "The photos of the date with my brother looked great. I even dined out at *Farina e Fiori* this week because of it."

"Then we did our job," Emma smiled. "And you are not the first person to tell me that. Not even the first person today."

She turned to Oliver. "I'll see you tomorrow?"

He nodded, and the knot in his stomach didn't know if it should be relieved or not. Before he could say anything else, they were interrupted by another couple who took the opportunity to talk with Emma, pulling her into the hall where some were still gathered.

"What's going on?" Victoria demanded.

"Not now, Viki."

"That didn't work on me growing up, and it isn't working now. Tell me as we walk home. Believe it or not, I am not a complete idiot."

Emma wasn't sure what to make of the day overall. "I can see the wheels turning," Anne said as they walked to their flats.

"I think it went well," Emma said slowly, letting the events of the morning percolate. "I mean, I talked with over a dozen people."

"Not including Oliver and his sister, yes. It was a great idea—for both of us," Anne agreed. "And I'm glad we went together just to make being stared at a bit easier. They've known us all our lives, yet it was like I suddenly sprouted a tail."

"They were just surprised the mayor deigned them with her presence," Emma rolled her eyes.

Anne bumped her shoulder against Emma's. "And still not a word about Oliver. My bait wasn't good enough."

"What do you want me to say? We said hello, I officially met his sister, she ate at *Farina e Fiori,* so your campaign did what it was suppose to do." She knew by the look Anne gave her that she didn't buy it. "It was their first public encounter since the date that wasn't held in my office or the police station, so I anticipated awkwardness. I think I over-anticipated the entire situation."

"You thought Oliver would embarrass you?"

"No. Not really. I don't know what I thought. If we didn't have a date in the morning and it was done after *Farina e Fiori,* I wouldn't even be thinking about it now."

"But you agreed to more dates. Four more!" The last ended with a bit of a squee which led to Emma pushing Anne as they approached their flats.

"Go home, idiot," she laughed.

She dumped her keys and purse on the table in the entrance and then took off her shoes. She was overthinking it and maybe not giving Oliver enough credit. He was younger than her, but not a child, far from it.

Just admit you're a tad bit scared and enjoy it, Emma told herself as she pulled out things to make lunch. Having what felt like an eager village collectively watching, like their new favorite reality show, didn't help. She didn't know what to expect when dating, period. She *really* didn't know what to expect when dating a younger man who was below her in the chain of command.

Chapter 6

Emma spotted Oliver when she stepped out of her car. "Hiya!" he waved, and the knot she'd spent the past twenty-four hours building began to unravel.

"I hope you weren't expecting a full English," Oliver said as she stepped on the sidewalk.

"Not at the café, no. Wait, were you?"

"No?"

She laughed and swore there was a bit of blush on his cheeks, although it could be the nip in the wind. The day would warm up, but the mornings and evenings were still cool. "I love this weather," Emma smiled as she walked in through the door Oliver opened.

"It suits you."

She raised an eyebrow as she grabbed a menu to hand him. "I already know what I'm going to have. Hi Amelia," Emma greeted the woman behind the counter who was the owner and pastry chef.

"I'll confess you had me do a double take. I was pretty sure we weren't selected for your date!" said Amelia.

"We'll take the table in the corner," Emma nodded, not acknowledging. She ordered all the seasonal dishes and an extra-large latte.

"You made it sound like you haven't been in before," Emma commented as they took seats at the table that was in the furthest corner. Anyone walking by could peek in the window and see them, but they were far enough away that most wouldn't notice a couple sitting down.

"I only seem to come in the afternoon for coffee and whatever pastries are left over from the morning," he admitted. "Wait, why?"

"You seem to know everyone," Emma pointed out. "At least in Ravenswick, and I'd guess half of the neighboring villages, too." He was friendly, affable, and good with people. Normally she'd think about that in the context of work—it made him good at what he did, and honestly something she could mold other departments to be—but this morning she found herself taking in Oliver the man, not the policeman.

"I know Amelia from church," he told her. "Her grandmother plays bridge with my grandmother. Left the village, like most do after high school, came back during Covid and decided to open up a café last year."

"You could put Dani, Charlie, Mrs. McCarthy—hell, all the village busybodies to shame with the amount of local gossip you have," Emma laughed as their breakfast was brought out.

"Hey!" he pouted and she found herself itching to touch his face, run her fingers through his hair. *Where did that come from, Emma?*

"You'll survive," she promised with a smile.

"I think they prefer to be called 'Village Godmothers.' Someone made the mistake of referring to Charlie as the village gossip."

"Who?"

"They've since moved; this was before you moved back," he grinned and she laughed, enjoying that he felt comfortable joking around with her.

She stabbed into her waffle loaded with seasonal fruit and a dusting of powder sugar. "I always forget how *huge* these are! Ignore me as I stuff my face," she warned him as she cut into her breakfast, missing his grin.

They ate and talked comfortably, ignoring the other patrons, although Emma was pretty sure more than the usual decided to eat indoors than have takeaway that day.

"What did you think of Reverend Paul?"

"That I want to be that fit and spry when I'm his age," Emma admitted. "Anne invited herself to come with me, at least this time, so I wasn't the only odd duckling there. Thank you."

"For what?"

"For how you handled seeing me there. I hope it wasn't awkward. It shouldn't have been awkward." Yet Emma worked up this knot in her chest over it, thinking about *what if* this and *what if* that. Theirs was one date with a promise of more, but that wasn't enough for them to not interact like she was his superior in public.

She was making it a bigger deal in her head after the fact than it actually had been, as far as she knew. She didn't actually know what was going on in Oliver's head.

"I was surprised, I'll admit that. I never expected to see you there. I'm assuming Mass was held at St Margaret's, even with the missing monstrance?"

"It was. We went to the *early* early morning Mass. The monstrance is for the side chapel for adoration. Or was. Adoration is still happening, just not with that particular monstrance," she explained. *Was she babbling? She was babbling. Pull it together, Em!* "Mrs. McCarthy decided to start doing adoration for Lent. Wednesday after evening Mass through Thursday Mass."

"That's where someone is always sitting in the chapel, right?"

Emma nodded. "One hour slots. I signed up for an hour, my sacrifice for Lent and all. Then Pope Francis died."

"I mean, I liked him but what does that have to do with it?"

"Mrs. McCarthy decided to keep it going through the mourning period and election of the next pope. And when she asked us to continue on?" she sighed dramatically.

"I don't think anyone can say 'no' to her," Oliver grinned.

"It would take a person with more will power than I," Emma agreed. "Part of my new role is community building and intercommunity building," Emma said quickly. "Since several of the other villages are even smaller—at least regarding the police force—building up relations with the community and between all of the stationhouses is important. So I'll be attending a service in each parish this month now that Easter is over to let the people see me," she explained. "Anne went since this is her patch as mayor. Dani," Emma said, naming the older woman who worked in her office as her liaison and part of the busybody group, "has arranged it with the other four mayors, too."

She looked at her watch and sighed, she never had enough time in the morning. "Here," Amelia appeared suddenly at their table with a takeaway box. "You always order more than you can eat in one setting," she laughed.

"Not my fault your portion sizes are more American than English!" Emma hollered at her when she walked off. "I should know."

She thought as she grabbed her takeaway coffee and breakfast leftovers that they probably looked like colleagues leaving, with Oliver in his police uniform and her in her blazer. *That's a good thing, right?* she asked herself.

"I'll see you later, chief super," Oliver promised, and she had the urge to pull him into a kiss, and the thought nearly made her blush. Instead, she let him open her car door since her hands were full and she sat down, putting the coffee in its slot, then the box carefully on her seat. She turned to look up at him as he leaned against her car door.

"That sounded like a promise, Barnes," she commented and leaned over to reach for her door handle. "I'm curious how you'll fulfill it," she teased as she pulled the door closed and reached for her seatbelt.

She managed to wait till she had straightened out and started down the street—with a glimpse of an amused Oliver in her rearview mirror—before laughing and wondering where the hell that came from.

"Like I know the rules," Emma shrugged, before grabbing her coffee to take a sip. Her total serious relationships in life were zero. She had the occasional date, but her ambition tended to scare off men and, honestly, she looked down on them for that.

Her phone rang as she pulled up to her office, and her sister's name popped up. "Rumor has it you two were at the café this morning," she said in way of greeting.

"You already knew we were having breakfast together."

"I did. Now the rest of Ravenswick does," Jane pointed out.

"It wouldn't exactly be possible to hide it, not here," Emma pointed out, waiting to exit her car. She didn't want anyone to get a hint of what their conversation was about.

"That makes me wonder if you would hide it?"

"Not from you. Hell, I was just thinking about how I need to probably ask you for advice as you have way more dating experience than I do. From the rest of the village though? That is a solid 'probably.'"

"I get that. As for the dating advice, you need only relax and enjoy yourself. You overthink too much. Good for your job, but not here. It's just Oliver."

"What does that mean?"

"I just mean, you're stepping out with one guy and he happens to be a sweetheart, so don't overthink his motives or anything. Anyway, off to teach. At least one of us started the day with Amelia's amazing waffle sunrise breakfast plate."

"Are there photos?!" How else did she know what Emma had.

"Not that I know of. *Ciao*."

"Rumor has it you had a date this morning," his partner Nancy greeted Oliver with a Cheshire grin.

"Rumors are already spreading?" he asked, only slightly surprised. "Whatever, let's start on those last two houses. If nothing is there, I'm out of ideas."

"As long as you aren't out of ideas on the dating front," Nancy grinned. "Rumor has it, it was cute, both of you going out before start of shift."

"Knock it off."

It was all bluster, no bite to his comment. "Good job. Seriously, Barnes. Alright, focus, work," she promised.

It was an hour into it when Oliver heaved a sigh. Even at two times the speed, watching videos was mind numbing.

"Finally!"

Oliver rolled his chair over to look, and she played it back.

Not the sharpest of cameras but a suspicious man with a sack definitely had what looked like the top of the monstrance sticking out of his sack. She paused it when he turned, and his face came into frame. "Who the hell is that?" Oliver wondered.

He may not know everyone in Ravenswick, like Emma claimed, but he knew most, and he certainly didn't know this guy.

"I'll catch up the inspector, you get started circulating his face, then," Nancy said as she stood.

For two days Emma heard about Oliver but managed to not see him. How, she had no clue. And everyone she did see, managed to give her a look that screamed *So you and young Oliver Barnes, huh?* Some of the more brazen asked how their dates—plural—had been and where the next one would be. Considering she worked nearly twelve hours both days piecing together a new initiative to propose to her superiors for recruitment and a social event for the villages —she was physically and mentally exhausted.

And responding back with *I wish I knew where the next one would be!* made her sound desperate.

So how she was convinced to grab a quick bite was lost on her. There would be nothing quick at the pub after work. She saved her work, shut down her computer, then grabbed her blazer. "See you tomorrow, Dani," Emma told her secretary as she shut her office door. "I'm assuming you passed along to Mrs. McCarthy the latest about the monstrance?"

"Of course." Dani didn't even bother to look up as she finished typing her own report, the question clearly not worth her time. Part of the same click as Mrs. McCarthy, Harry, and Charlie, she'd become an expert in the last few decades on information that could be passed along to her friends.

She turned as Emma began to walk away. "A reminder that you have a conference call with all the DIs in the morning at 9 am, and a meeting at HQ at 1."

With a sigh, Emma gave a wave as she walked out. The pub was close enough she could walk, so she decided to stretch her legs. As her eyes adjusted, she saw the girls at a table across the room, waving when they caught sight of her.

"Really? Wednesday?" Emma drawled as she took the last empty chair.

"What? Who wants to cook midweek?" Anne said.

"We've heard good things about the fish stew they've added," Catherine said.

"I have my shift for adoration in the morning," Emma reminded them. The Monstrance may be missing, but Ms. McCarthy wouldn't let that stop her from ensuring a church event continued on.

"You said Thursday," Anne said, confused.

"Yeah, 4 am," Emma pointed out. "That's still Thursday."

"No one forced you," Jane pointed out.

Literally everyone in the group chat enthusiastically jumped on board the idea of eating out to try out the pub's new meal—and help with Anne's mayoral campaign promise to boost local business. She didn't want to be the only one *not* to go out.

"It's just been a day. Did you all order already?"

"Just drinks. Henry!" Maryanne waved over the worker.

"Just soda for me. And this fish stew everyone's talking about," Emma ordered, and the other girls placed their dinner orders.

She saw the way her sister and Catherine seemed to zero in on the entrance at the same time. "What? Cute guy or something?"

"Something," Jane agreed as Catherine snorted into her drink. Emma looked over her shoulder and saw Oliver enter with his partner, Nancy Halliwell, another PC named Namrata Bakshi, and their DS, Fanny Fletcher. She saw them grab a table on the other side of the bar and she felt her body relax.

"What?" Maryanne asked. She was sitting next to Emma, noticed her reaction.

"This is why I said no to the pubs. What's it like if the ones you supervise come in to socialize? They can't relax, let loose, if I'm here. Then it makes it awkward for everyone," Emma said.

"I think you're underestimating Oliver." Jane shook her head.

Emma didn't say anything as their food came. She didn't want anyone else to overhear them but didn't know how to explain it to them. Catherine, as chief of the fire department, was the only one to understand rank in a way similar to her.

She still couldn't help herself and stole a look across the bar. Oliver looked up at the same time, a smile on his face as he made eye contact. She subtly tipped her glass in his direction before taking a drink.

"I'm off," Emma said as she finished the stew. "It's a long day and starts early."

"Next week we'll do takeouts on Thursday night," Jane promised.

"I could have said no," Emma said. "Sorry about my mood, just a long day. See you all later."

She could have said no. She was a big girl; she knew life would go on if she skipped their weekly meal out. So the question was, why didn't she beg off this time?

She caught Oliver's eye as she pulled open the door to leave. Her heart skipped a beat.

That's why.

Chapter 7

Dani wasn't known for pulling punches, which Emma appreciated. She clicked off the virtual meeting with the five Detective Inspectors under her command and looked up to the older woman expectantly. She didn't know how the woman had been with previous commanders, but she didn't shy away from sharing her opinion with Emma.

Emma hoped that meant she trusted her and wanted Emma to succeed.

"Edmund Reeve has always been an ass."

Emma snorted. "Is that what we're calling sexist now?" She didn't know for sure but suspected the DI had applied for her position and was denied.

He made his disdain for Emma clear.

"If he was sexist, I'd say that," Dani said through pursed lips. "You have an hour before you have to leave for HQ."

They both turned when one of the office interns knocked on the door. "Ma'am, someone dropped this off for you. From the café." She gently handed it over and went back to her desk where Emma had no doubt she'd soon be talking about it.

The box was four inches by four inches, with a little piece of paper featuring her name taped to the top. She gently peeled off the sticker to open it and just looked at the cupcake inside.

"There's a note, not that I need it," Dani said amused. She pointed to the paper with her name. Emma pulled it off and saw it had writing on the back.

You didn't have dessert last night.

Ollie

"What the hell?"

"I believe that is what people would call 'sweet,'" Dani said amused.

"Sergeant, out. Lunch," Emma ordered.

Dani stood and opened the door. "Ma'am. Nothing wrong with sweet," she added as she pulled the door shut behind her, choking back a laugh.

She purposefully didn't look at Emma as she turned to walk away, avoiding her glare. Emma turned back to the cupcake at hand. "What am I going to do with you?" she sighed. "Well, *you* specifically I will eat." Dessert was never a no, after all. The memory made her blush, which just further embarrassed her.

There was nothing wrong with sweet, she repeated to herself. She just wasn't use to it, had no experience with someone trying to be sweet to her.

She opened her desk drawer and grabbed the fork from her emergency stash for days she brought lunch but forgot to bring cutlery. Stuffing her face was hardly professional and she had to leave for a meeting with her bosses. The last thing she needed was to get lemon cupcake on her.

First things first, she decided, and texted Oliver.

> *Thank you for the cupcake.*

His reply was immediate.

> *You didn't have dessert.*

She rolled her eyes; his note said as much. Before she could think what to respond, he sent another.

> *Are you free Saturday for lunch?*

Before she could think—more specifically, before she could overthink—she responded back with yes.

> *I'll pick you up at 11:30*

Deciding not to overthink, she just replied "see you then" and took a giant bite of the cupcake, the lemon bursting over her tongue. Did he know she loved lemon, or was it a lucky guess? Either way, she savored every bite.

She heard the car door and looked out her bedroom window, which on the second story faced out the back and gave her a view of her garden—well, where her garden would be one day—and the lane. She saw Oliver walking towards her back door and put in the earrings she had picked out right before he arrived.

Not fancy—the Chinese restaurant was the last one left in Ravenswick for them to go to—but she wanted to wear something cute. A new blouse with jeans and jewelry and she almost felt like a new person.

"Just enjoy yourself, Emma," she reminded her reflection as she walked out of her room to go answer the door.

She opened the door to Oliver who also wore jeans with a button down, and she decided she very much enjoyed seeing Oliver in civilian clothes.

"You look amazing."

Emma smiled and motioned for him to come in. "I need to grab my purse, but I'm ready to go."

"About that."

She turned to look at him as she grabbed her purse. She went with one her sister gave her, a small bag with a chain because it was cute and she never had the chance to use it.

"I have a surprise. You won't hate it," he promised.

She raised an eyebrow. "What kind of surprise? Like, a cupcake or a special menu?" she wondered.

He held the door open for her and then stepped aside so she could lock up.

He got in his seat and started the car while she buckled up. "You vetoed the two pubs in Ravenswick," he reminded her as he buckled his own belt before turning the car around in the lane to exit back down the way he'd driven in, their little lane ending at her unit.

"And?"

"You never vetoed the idea of four dates," he grinned as he turned onto the small road that then connected to the main street. In this direction they would leave Ravenswick in a couple miles and be headed towards the next village, Thorndale.

"And?" she turned towards him in her seat. "Chinese was the other direction, so where are you taking me?"

"Have you been to the Indian place in Seabrook?"

Seabrook? That was two villages over, and the furthest west in her new jurisdiction. "Of course. I did an observational period in Seabrook's police station, like all of my new command."

"What did you think of it?"

"If I said I hated it, then what?"

"There's an American grill also in Seabrook. Or the pub in Thorndale, but I figured that was too similar to going to a pub here, so the reasons for skipping the pubs here probably applied."

"Thorndale does need more food options, but it is small."

"Their mom-and-pop restaurant never reopened after Covid, sadly," Oliver said. "But Indian is okay?"

"Absolutely. The food was great when I was there. Have you been?"

"Once. Victoria wanted to go when they opened. She'll bring me food on the rare occasion she has to head over there." He took a quick glance when they came to a stop at an intersection passing through Thorndale . "What do you think of Thorndale?"

"If you mean the village, its nice. If you mean the constabulary, there's some changes to be made."

He grinned as he drove through the village. "I'm hoping you like us the best."

"I technically can't have favorites."

"On paper," he grinned. "Okay, no work talk, sorry. I've heard about the DI here, which is what made me think of it. Do you miss living in London?"

The change surprised her, but the topic surprised her even more. Mostly because she hadn't thought of London in ages, and she knew Oliver was a Raven through and through. He might move somewhere else, but he wouldn't be happy in the big city.

Where did that come from? She wondered. She felt her impression was true from everything she knew about him, even if they never talked about London or city living before.

"I enjoyed it, but I think I always knew I was there for a purpose. That it was a stop for me," she admitted. "There are things I love, don't get me wrong. The girls and I are going to spend a weekend just doing touristy things next month. But unless the job takes me back there, I don't think I'll live there again."

They pulled up in front of the Indian restaurant, and she took another look at it. The paint job was new—that alone made it stand out in Seabrook. It had some decals on the door when you approached, but otherwise the building itself was understated until you walked in and there was an explosion of color from the booths to the flooring to the pillars.

After they'd eaten, Oliver watched as Emma whispered to their waitress on her way to the restroom. She returned the same time the waitress did who handed her a bag that had a package of naan and humus.

"It's an apology to the girls. I was a bit crabby to them when we went out this week," Emma explained as she handed the waitress her card. He felt conflicted when she insisted on paying but decided she was a professional woman, she wasn't doing it to hurt his pride.

He'd also thought he'd be insistent when they were out in Ravenswick and pay for them, so he would think about it later when he had time to himself. Right now, he had a wonderful hour with Emma and wanted to drag it out.

"Do you have to be back anytime?" he asked as he opened her car door.

"No. You?"

"Day off. Want to take a walk?" While not quite on the sea, Seabrook set on an inlet that had a walking path which, if he'd heard correctly, had great views.

"Sure," she agreed. It only took a few minutes to find a place to park off the walking trail. "Where are you going to church this weekend?" he asked. "For your Grand Tour."

If she was surprised, he remembered she didn't show it. "Going West to East so starting with Seabrook. Then Thorndale , then Brackenmoor, and finally Littleton. Anne set a precedent, the mayors are attending with me at each."

"At least you won't be alone."

"Hmm. Alone doesn't bother me," she admitted. "There's a lot about this job that requires teamwork or leadership but, well, the process of getting here was me alone. Finding which opportunities worked best, applying for them, moving for them, being the only woman to have that position before in the area sometimes."

He was reminded that this was only a two-year position for her, a step on her ladder. Where would she go next? Part of him was curious, part of him didn't want to think about her leaving. "What do you want to do? I guess I'm asking where does this all lead for you?"

"Have you always wanted to be a cop?" she asked him.

"Mostly. I fluctuated between cop and fireman as a kid. Ultimately, I wanted to do something in the community, and I think I saw my options as cop, fireman, or clergy. Never really saw myself as a member of the clergy."

She laughed as he smiled. "Growing up I wanted to be the Sheriff of Nottingham. I don't know where or why, but it's always been what I wanted. My cousin and I were obsessed with Robin Hood. My mother remembers clear as a bell me saying that things would have been better if the Sheriff of Nottingham had been a girl. Mind you, this goes back to the cartoon version."

"Where they're animals?" he grinned.

"My cousin and I could quote that movie. Jane too, although she was more interested in the Robin Hood and Maid Marion storyline. But I've just always known. My cousin is a cop. Neither of our families are surprised," she laughed. "So maybe not Nottingham, but one day High Sheriff."

He grinned because he could see her doing that.

"Anne wants to be the Lord Lieutenant to my High Sheriff. We'll get there."

"I don't doubt either of you. Where's your cousin?" he asked. He had never heard of her having a cousin on the force.

"Los Angeles."

"What?"

She laughed. "My uncle went to graduate school in Texas. Married my now-aunt. They had two daughters. The eldest is a year younger than me—Eleanor."

He shot her a look of disbelief. "Another Austen?"

"My aunt said she was not going to have her American daughters feel less than, and I think my Aunt was a bit obsessed with the film. The one with Alan Rickman. Also one of my favorite Sheriff of Nottingham," she said. My younger cousin is Mary. She's an ER nurse."

"No one in your family does anything by halves."

She smiled. "I'm proud of us. All of us—there's a couple more," she promised. "Although we are the only two cops."

They paused at a bend in the path and she leaned her hip against the railing as she turned to look at him. "Let me ask you something, Have you thought about becoming a sergeant?"

He glanced away for a second to gather his thoughts, then turned to look back at her. Would his answer change anything between them? He feared his answer wouldn't impress her.

"Honestly, no. I enjoy my job, being out and about in the community. Most days, anyway. Once you start moving up, though, the job becomes more about paperwork than policing. I can't remember the last time my DI was in the field."

"Hey." She took his hand in hers and he stared at their hands for a moment. "I was just curious. Promise," she said, giving his hand a gentle squeeze. "There's room in your office in terms of budget for one more sergeant. If you don't want it, I'm nearly certain your partner will. The only rank I care about is mine."

He nodded and decided to believe her. He agreed that Nancy would probably apply for the promotion.

Just don't think about the rest, he told himself. The rest being if Emma really was just curious, and if she judged him now because of his answer.

He realized she'd never let go of his hand. He rubbed his thumb along the back of her hand and waited to see what she would do. She didn't jerk away, so he turned to lean against the railing, their bodies parallel as they faced each other.

She said, "Catherine will want to know why you decided against being a fireman."

He grinned, not expecting this return to their previous conversation. "I don't have an answer. I think I just decided cops were cooler at some point."

Emma laughed. "She is going to hate that answer, but I have to agree with you."

The moment was perfect, and he thought, *what the hell?* He brought his other hand up to cup her face, and after the smallest hesitation, she leaned into it.

"Oliver."

"Yes."

"Kiss me already so I can stop wondering."

"Yes ma'am." He closed the distance between them, letting go of her hand so he could wrap his arm around her waist.

Chapter 8

Emma braced herself as Jane knocked on Anne's door. "How bad do you think it went?" Jane wondered.

"The fact that she didn't say *anything* afterwards is what has me nervous," Maryanne admitted, the three of them piled onto the back steps.

Emma sighed. "Naan and humus is not going to be enough." She had just turned down their alley when Jane texted, saying that no one had talked to Anne since her date the previous night. She clearly was home but not talking to anyone. So all of them had agreed to gang up on her.

Catherine pulled into her designated spot and ran over to join them. "I grabbed a couple pints." She held up the bag from the grocers, along with ice cream.

Maryanne pulled out her key to let them in just as Anne opened the door.

"What?" Anne asked.

"Hello to you, too," Maryanne said and pushed inside, the others following suit.

"You had your date last night, and no word?" Maryanne demanded. "It seems only fair after we grilled Emma to hear about yours."

"I one thousand percent agree," Emma laughed. "I brought naan. It's fresh. Cat got ice cream."

"Naan? From where?" Anne asked. "And there's nothing to say. You can see from the photos it was a nice dinner."

"In his lordship's *home*," Catherine pointed out. "But wait, where did you get the naan? That is *not* from the market."

"It's from the restaurant in Seabrook," Emma said. She jerked back the bag from Anne who was about to tease her. "Nope. This is about you. And his lordship."

"He is as insufferable as he was when we were in high school. Which goes to show how insufferable he is, since we didn't go to school with him in our humble public school and yet still knew about him."

Emma and Catherine shared a look. Everyone knew that anyone who was anyone went to the posh private school an hour away. The super posh, like the Baron's family, went away to boarding school.

But he had always been home for summers, and he ran in the same local circle as Anne's family, who were well-known in the horse world.

"Well, remember it is for a good cause," Catherine said finally. "Rumor has it he calmed down after his parents' died and he assumed the title."

No matter what, Anne refused to go into details. "If you're my friend you'll change the topic and distract me," she told Emma.

Emma broke off a piece of bread. "Like about our first kiss? Someone seriously explain to me what the hell I'm doing, because I am his superior."

"What if the roles were reversed? I mean if the man was the superior. It's not like there's not precedent," Jane pointed out.

"We don't work together. Otherwise, it's just a matter of paperwork," Emma said. "It's only been two dates. The blind date doesn't count," she added quickly. She sighed as she ripped another piece of bread off. "I don't know what I'm doing."

Jane and Anne shared a look. "What do you think you're doing wrong?" Jane asked. "Because it's still new and fresh."

"There's nothing to do wrong. Oliver's not an ass like his lordship. He's not going to intentionally hurt you," Anne pointed out.

Catherine, who was sitting on the floor near Emma's legs, leaned back against the couch. "You have always put relationships aside. Nothing wrong with that," she added quickly. "But you didn't do any of the embarrassing, dumb stuff when you were young."

"Just means she's older and wiser and can avoid the young, dumb stuff," Maryanne countered.

"Like what? Concrete examples," Emma asked.

"Communication," Jane said. "Specifically, how important it is to communicate."

"And realizing when he's trying to take away your boundaries," Maryanne added. Anne wrapped an arm around her sister, resting her head on her shoulder.

"You did realize," Anne pointed out. "And you got out."

"Good riddance," Jane agreed.

"I just keep thinking about how he's twenty-eight and I'm thirty-six. I know, I'm not old," she said quickly before Anne could interject. "But remember when we were in our twenties?"

"You knew what you wanted and worked to get there," Catherine pointed out. "Nothing wrong with that."

"No, but there were consequences to that decision, about the direction of my life and what my life looks like now." She sighed as she got a text. "Gotta go," she sighed. She stepped outside to take the call from Dani.

And was really glad Maryanne wasn't around to hear.

"Officers responded to a domestic," Dani said, referring to a domestic violence call. "Ultimately they can't do anything, but it was in Ravenswick so I'm giving you a heads up."

"Officers are okay?" Domestic violence could turn dangerous for cops quickly.

"Shaken up, frustrated, but fine."

"Thanks, Dani. See you Monday." She disconnected and decided to head over to her flat. She wanted to enjoy the remnants of her date without the post-date analysis or advice. She asked for the advice but would think about it later. Right now she wanted to bask a little more.

Oliver arrived at the station on Monday. It was the first time he had seen his partner since Friday. "Hey, I heard about the domestic. You okay?"

"Frustrated as hell. PC Bakshi was there; it was her first. Not that we get many." Nancy sighed. "But I told the woman I'd do more foot patrols in the area."

"Course," Oliver said and grabbed his hat.

"If you swing by the café I'll take a latte," Charlie said from her desk as they walked out. "Or a cupcake!"

Oliver blushed as they walked out. Nancy bumped against him. "Ignore her. It was sweet."

"I know." Oliver smiled. "Rumor has it you signed up for the next sergeant exams."

"Yeah. Would it be weird to have me as your superior?"

"I'll get over it."

"You don't mind? I thought we might have to fight over it. I overheard the sergeants talking about how the station has the go ahead to recruit one more."

"Why would I mind?" he asked.

"Because you're dating the chief super," Nancy pointed out.

"Doesn't change what I want. Or don't want, in this case. Is that wrong?"

Nancy shot him a look, concern coloring her face. "Why would it be wrong? Did Charlie say something?"

"No." They had reached the neighborhood of the DV and just continued looping around the village. They bumped into people, stopping to talk with everyone.

It made it closer to an hour before they looped back around and reached the café. They were exiting the café, Oliver holding the door for Nancy who had her drink and Charlie's, when he saw Emma approaching the café.

"Chief super, ma'am," Nancy said surprised.

Emma eyed the cups. "That looks like Charlie's latte. Rumor has it she manages to get someone to get her one daily."

"She brings goodies for the station house, so it evens out," Oliver said easily.

"Officer Halliwell, actually, I was going to email you. I'm hoping you and DS Fletcher will swing by my office," she told Nancy, surprising her.

"Yes ma'am, of course."

"Excellent."

Oliver took a step back to reach for the door for her. "Ma'am."

Emma's smile was genuine, and that alone made whatever gossip might arise worth it. "Barnes."

"Was that awkward for you?" Nancy whispered as they reached the end of the block.

"No. Why?"

"I guess I just thought it might be, having to act like you're not dating." She shrugged. "You know you'll need to fill out the paperwork sooner rather than later, right?"

"We haven't talked about it. It's been just a couple dates."

"But you want to have more. And she hasn't said no to more," Nancy pointed out. She

paused when they reached the station house. "What you said before. Has she said anything about you being a constable?"

"No. I guess...let's say the roles were reversed and you were dating a chief super," he said. "It wouldn't look wrong in that case. The man is the one with the superior position."

"People would be more concerned over whether he used that authority over me," Nancy pointed out. "Which is why I am *very* much not interested in dating a cop, ever. But I see your point. As long as she's not pressuring you to do something you don't want to do, Oliver. That's the point. She is ahead of you, which means she has power and influence over you. As long as it is *your* decision, who cares? The important thing is you're happy. I'd have to be dead to not see that." She nodded for him to get the door for her.

He was happy, but he worried his lack of ambition would be an issue in the future.

"Oliver." Nancy interrupted his thoughts. "Focus. Next date." she insisted before going to give Charlie her coffee.

Chapter 9

"Date number three," Emma mused as Oliver shut her door. "Chinese, or another surprise?"

"A surprise," he said, smiling. "I do recall you saying you wanted to see what I'd do."

Emma laughed and grabbed her phone. "Rumor has it your roommate, James, is doing this motorcycle race next month."

"He never grew out of his daredevil phase," Oliver said. "He also swears it is a totally legit and legal race as he wouldn't put me in the awkward position of having to arrest him."

"Good to know. I think he works on bikes?"

"Mechanic, work on most things," he said as they turned out onto the main road. They drove through the village before coming out on the eastern side.

"So not Thorndale or Seabrook," Emma wondered.

"I thought a bit farther," he admitted. "Preston is outside your jurisdiction."

"It's like an hour away," Emma said, surprised.

"Too far?"

"I'm just surprised, is all."

"I figured that gives us plenty of time to talk." He shot her a grin that was just so easy and happy, she was pretty sure she returned it with a goofy one. He was genuinely happy to spend time with her. *That's the point, Em.*

She leaned back as the scenery went by. "Well, what do you want to talk about, then?" she wondered aloud, acting nonchalant. He snorted which made her laugh. "Do you do motorcycle races?"

"Not race, no. I've ridden them."

"Past tense?"

"Had to respond to a motorcycle accident. Pretty much ruined them for me," he admitted.

"Yeah, I get that." Emma nodded. "We all have something the job seems to ruin. Surely James has also seen accidents."

"Probably, but usually the bike afterwards, not the remains of the person." He saw her confused look. "He somehow developed a reputation for helping family members sell the bikes, or parts that were salvageable. He fixes them up and finds a new buyer or sells for parts. The family doesn't have to deal with it."

"That's actually really sweet and ingenious. Are he and Victoria dating?" Emma asked.

"What? Hell no. They'd murder each other. Why?"

"Just curious. Brother's best friend always around? Seems like they should have at some point."

"No."

His assertiveness on the matter made her laugh. "I'm sure you're right, I don't know either of them."

She got a text and checked her phone. He saw her smile and wanted to know what made her happy.

"What is it?" he asked.

"My cousin. In Los Angeles. She's got the approval we need."

"We?"

"Oh, I assumed it was known," Emma said bewildered. "Working vacation. Jane and I are going to L.A. Our cousin scored tickets to *the* concert of the decade at the stadium. We're flying out for the concert and then I'm staying on for a couple weeks. An international exchange, if you will." Emma laughed. "I'll be talking about our model of community policing to the LAPD and whomever they invited, and riding along with my cousin."

He looked at her, surprised. "How is no one talking about this? Rumors spread as easy as breathing in Ravenswick, but I haven't heard a whisper of this."

"The idea was from my superiors, who worked it out with the LAPD. So maybe because no one in my office is actually handling this." Emma shrugged.

"When do you leave?"

"In a month, and I'll be gone for two weeks. The concert is on a Saturday, and Jane will fly back on Sunday so she only has to miss Monday for work."

"This is your cousin who is a cop? Eleanor?" He grinned.

"Yes." Emma smiled as they arrived into the city. He always paid attention when she talked and remembered what she said. Granted, being named after Jane Austen characters made remembering easier. But Oliver made everything so easy that time just flew by. She wanted to savor every moment.

She watched him navigate traffic. "You have a plan," she accused.

"Not a plan—a suggestion. There's a new place that just opened with great reviews. This American food critic on social media tried it and raved about them. It was all over all of my social media feeds and the food looked great. I figured we'd check it out." He grinned impishly. "But Preston will have a ton of food options. I figured we could just drive around till we find something you want."

She took his hand resting on the gearshift and brought it up to kiss the back of it. "You are a sweetheart."

His slight blush was endearing. "Let's see if the Yankee was right," she decided and watched him park, engraving this moment in her memory. She had seen enough examples of bad relationships in this job to realize Oliver was an absolute gift.

Once they settled in their seats after ordering food he said, "It doesn't sound like this is your first trip to America."

"No. We would take a trip out there once a year or so growing up, and my uncle and aunt would come here once a year, once he finished graduate school. I think I was about five the first time they made it back to England. It's harder now—tickets have gone up astronomically. But you don't turn down these concert tickets."

"So I've heard."

"Our other cousin actually got tickets to her tour stop in London, too, for the month after I get back. Enough for all six of us cousins to go together," she said excitedly. "We haven't done anything all together since before Covid."

"Aren't the other Austen Saints going to be jealous?" he teased.

"Absolutely. Can't be helped." Emma grinned unapologetically as their food arrived. "So if you don't listen to the biggest singer on the planet, what do you listen to?"

"I don't *not* listen to her, but I also won't be heartbroken about missing her concert. I'm more a rock or country person."

She stared at him in surprise. "Rock *and* country?"

"Eclectic—what can I say? My parents had very different tastes, so I grew up listening to both. And whatever pop sensation Victoria was into at the moment."

"Is she into K-pop? Because I'm beginning to think I have more in common with your sister when it comes to music." Emma laughed. "At least we have movies and books."

"Speaking of, did you see the latest Agatha Christie being made into a series?"

Three days later Oliver found himself in his apartment, wallowing, with his sister over for dinner while Emma was at a work dinner back up near Preston.

Oliver knew one more date wasn't enough with Emma. He wasn't sure he had convinced her, though.

"Earth to Ollie"

Oliver looked up at his sister.

"I can see you are distracted." She set aside her plate. "Just tell her. You clearly want to see more of her after your fourth date."

"Sorry. I know I'm not the greatest company right now."

"That's obvious. Less obvious is *why*—hence me asking."

With a sigh he opened his social media app to show the photo Emma had been tagged in earlier this evening. A work dinner with her colleagues and superiors up near headquarters, everyone in their formal uniforms.

"Okay. You're sad you're not there as her arm candy," Victoria guessed.

"Vicki!"

"I'm not a psychic, Ollie. So what's wrong?"

"She could hardly bring me as her plus one, could she?"

"I mean, I don't think it's a plus one type of event, and she might think it's only been three dates, since you insist on not counting the blind date..." she trailed off.

He ran his hands through his hair and finally voiced the thoughts that had crept up on him in the quiet moments. "Everyone would judge her for being with me. Because of the age difference and because I'm just a PC."

"So you're going to wallow, then" Victoria rolled her eyes. "Self-pity is the answer."

"How are you always such a downer in my time of need? It's a talent."

"Look," Victoria said and turned to face him. "I'm not saying it won't happen. But it has happened enough in the opposite direction it shouldn't be an issue. At least the age thing. You both met as adults, started seeing each other as adults. No one can claim she was some sort of groomer. I mean, did you even talk growing up? I don't recall."

"No." The age difference was big enough when they were growing up that she had gone to college by the time he'd become interested in girls and started dating. "The fact is, though, that she is the older one and that is unusual."

"She's also old enough to know what does or does not make her comfortable. If she didn't want to deal with it, she would call off your dates. Or just ghost you. She hasn't, which is encouraging."

"Okay, now you are less of a bratty sister. Thanks."

"You're both adults. Talk to her. She strikes me as the type to know her own mind."

His sister's advice percolated in the back of his mind while he showered later that night. Now was not the time to talk about all of that, but he didn't want her to *not* be thinking about him. So he texted.

> You looked amazing in your dress uniform tonight.

He wasn't sure when the dinner was over and was slightly surprised she texted back only a couple of minutes later.

> Was just thinking about you.

Praying that was a good sign, he replied with:

> hopefully good thoughts. how'd it go?

> How they always go. You know, to be fair, we really should put the pubs down on our list

He sat on his bed, goofily grinning. She texted back again before he could think of a response.

> Still don't think after work is a great time, though.

> Leave it to me, just tell me what you like from them and I'll handle the rest.

He laughed at her reply of

> promises promises.

They were squeezing in more dates, she was thinking of him—even before he texted her. The night was definitely ending on a high note.

Oliver got a head nod from the barman before he went in the back. He came back out with two bags of takeaway food.

"Rumor has it it's for a hot date with the chief super. What, we don't warrant a proper date?" the barman, named Henry, teased.

"I'm trying to impress her, you git. Hard to do with half the village in for dinner," Oliver joked as he handed over his card to pay. He grabbed the food and checked the time. Just enough to get back and take a quick shower. He felt like he was floating as he passed through the pub, saying hi to everyone he knew which felt like all the patrons. *All the more reason not to come in person,* he decided.

Definitely not in person, he thought, seeing his DI and DS placing an order on the other side of the bar. They were at least kind enough to not tease him, although they'd get their barbs in tomorrow, and he didn't care. He was excited about the idea of Emma coming over to his place, and if the date went well, which it should, he didn't care if the whole village gave him grief tomorrow.

He took a quick look around the place—making his fifth mental reminder to thank his sister for helping him tidy up—when the doorbell rang.

Suddenly, he was nervous. James had cleared up so he knew it would be just them, but maybe this was a bad idea. After all, he was living on a PC salary and had a roommate.

"Shit," Oliver said as he ran to the door.

Don't leave her stranded on the doorstep for everyone to see, he chastised himself.

He opened the door and everything simply stopped. She had changed after work into a dress that ended mid-thigh, and he suddenly wanted to pet her to see if it was as soft as it looked. Her hair, normally pulled back in a low bun, was let loose. She was very clearly just Emma St. George tonight.

"Can I come in?" Emma smiled and he nearly tripped over his feet as he jumped backwards.

"Shit, yeah. Bloody hell, you just sucker-punched me, is all," he said, holding the door open wide for her.

Her laughter trickled over him and he felt himself relaxing. "Hi," she said and leaned up to kiss him on the cheek.

He flipped the door closed and turned to capture her lips in a proper kiss, his hands wrapping around her. "Hi." He grinned as he rested his head against hers. "This dress is amazing. How the hell is it so soft?"

Emma laughed as she stepped back. "It smells good in here."

"Hungry? The food should be reheated by now."

"Famished. I worked through lunch and ate at my desk, which would've been fine, except I went off without my afternoon snack." She saw him frown as he pulled out a chair for her. "I'm hardly wasting away, constable."

"I think you're beautiful," he promised. He kissed her cheek, then turned to pull out the plates he was rewarming. "I take no credit but will pass along compliments to the chef."

She smiled when he pulled out the slices of chocolate cake for dessert, and he was pretty certain in that moment Emma was the only one for him. Not that he would ever say that out loud, but she was gorgeous, capable, and despite the fact that she could take care of herself, she enjoyed the simple pleasures with him; she appreciated his gestures.

When he took their plates to the sink, she stood to stretch her legs and headed to his living room. "What's James up to tonight?"

"Honestly, don't know. Didn't ask. He's a big boy."

Emma rolled her eyes. "Boys. Meanwhile, we all have our location sharing on with each other. Me and the Austen Saints," she clarified. "Even though I am the big scary chief super."

"Who would dare say scary?" he demanded and pulled her down onto his lap.

"Superlatives, sir," she teased as she adjusted so she leaned against the arm of the couch, her legs draped over his lap. "Kick ass does feel more appropriate."

"Much more appropriate," he agreed before leaning over to close the distance between them. "I am very quickly becoming addicted to this dress."

"Who knew you would have such a sensory reaction?" She smiled in wonder. Then all thoughts went away as all of his senses were simply filled with Emma.

Chapter 10

"You are a lifesaver," Emma told Jane as she grabbed the last of her things on her desk. It was somehow the end of day—she never had enough hours, it seemed—and if she hurried, she could shower and change before Oliver came over. It seemed only fair to have dinner at her place so they didn't have to kick James out again, and since they were getting food from the pub, she didn't have to cook. Since she'd had a full day from the moment she'd walked in the door, she didn't have the energy to do more than carry a takeaway bag.

"I am a saint, don't you know." Jane's laughter trickled over the phone. "I love it. God bless whoever came up with the idea of the Austen Saints. Anyway, my pleasure. You can help me do a mad dash cleaning when I find a guy."

"Done," Emma promised as she reached her car and it clicked over to her Bluetooth setting. "I'm about to pick up food, and I'll even get you a slice of cake as a thank-you."

"I'm happy for you, Em," Jane said, surprising her. "I didn't know what would happen after that blind date, but I'm happy he makes you happy."

"I'm happy I'm happy too," Emma said as she looped around to the pub. "I mean, I'm surprised like anyone else, but I'm happy."

"Good. Now rush," Jane said.

Emma saw the time, clicked to disconnect the call, and then looked for a parking spot. She would think about it later, because the fact was, she was on cloud nine. Who'd have thought? She and Oliver had managed at least one date a week for the month and a half after their blind date. Now look at them. She'd had no expectations about her love life when she'd moved back home, and now every time her phone chimed with a message, she hoped it was Oliver Barnes.

She grabbed the food and made it home in less than twenty minutes. The time crunch meant she couldn't overthink things.

Enjoy yourself, Emma. He's proving to be more than you could ever have imagined.

The truth of that stray thought struck her. She didn't ever imagine a world where she would go out with Oliver Barnes, let alone a world she looked forward to spending time with him.

She'd pushed through work so she could leave on time to get ready for tonight.

He knocked as she was lighting some candles. After she opened the door, she stilled, taking in the sight before her, seeing him there with a single rose.

"Do you want to come in?" she asked.

"One day I will stop being dumbstruck," he promised.

"I hope not." Emma smiled as she took the rose from him.

"Good, because that was a bald-faced lie. I can try to hide it better."

"Or don't." She recognized what Anne had called the hearts in his eyes, and it was such a boost to her ego. "I could definitely use the boost to my ego. Hungry?"

"And curious. Want me to pour?" he asked, seeing the wine. He did so as she grabbed the plates and followed her to her little dining table.

"How was your day?" she wondered aloud. "Not asking as the chief super," she added quickly.

"I know. And honestly, uneventful. Dead ends everywhere on the monstrance. We do extra patrols around the flats that had the domestic, and I can tell Nancy is frustrated. Hell, I'm frustrated."

"I get that. Charlie still getting her lattes?"

"Not every day, but often enough she's in a halfway decent mood." Oliver grinned. "What about you?"

"My recruitment campaign is approved, and we got the budget I wanted. Now to conscript people into helping." Emma sighed in relief. "Starting with your partner and DS Fletcher.

The social gathering budget—apparently we can't call it a party—is not as great as I had hoped."

"What campaign?"

"Across all five station houses, women only average 12% of officers and community support officers. Less than the national average, which they are also trying to increase. I need to bring in more women. Who better to recruit than other women?"

"You should do some too, you realize," he pointed out. "You're the highest-ranking woman in this part of England. Who better for girls to look up to than you?"

She smiled as she shook her head. "It's been pointed out. Realistically I know I'll have to, but I'm also doing enough press it isn't hard to find things about me. I want to highlight the other women from the area who are in the force."

"They look up to you, too."

Now she was the one blushing.

It wasn't until they moved to her living room after dinner he asked, "why do you need a boost to your ego?"

"Who doesn't?"

"You are amazing. Surely you know that. You're flying through the ranks."

"There's more to life than work, you know," she drawled. "At least that's what I've been told."

"Hey, no judgement," Oliver promised and turned to face her more directly on the couch.

"Surely the village gossip mill has talked about me. I grew up here," Emma pointed out. His confused face made her blush. "I don't date. Everyone has to know that."

"I didn't. Like, by choice? I'm honored."

"Hardly. By choice I mean," she said quickly. "I didn't ever really click with boys growing up. God, I can't believe I'm talking about this."

"Hey, it's okay," Oliver promised. "I have dated. All that means is it's a one-sided exchange of dating history."

She gave him a poignant look. "Come on. No one is that blasé about the whole thing."

"What does it matter?"

"You don't find it odd I haven't been in a serious relationship before?"

"Ever?" She shook her head. "It's unusual, but I don't see how it changes anything now," Oliver said. Every instinct told her he meant it, but she didn't know how that could be.

"Hey, I'll be the first to admit boys are dumb," Oliver told her and took one hand in his. In all this, he never shifted away from her, never tried to put distance between them.

"At some point I did stop; stopped looking, stopped thinking about it."

"Now this makes me feel special." He grinned. "The one who got you to think about it. Don't worry—secret's safe with me."

She snorted. "As if. It's Ravenswick. I'm surprised everyone isn't already talking about it."

"For the most part, I like to think they know to leave people alone when it matters. Besides, how would anyone know? It's not like someone kept a blog of your dating life while traveling around the country for work."

"It would have been very boring. Never went beyond a third date."

"It doesn't change how I see you, Em." Oliver smiled and leaned forward to gently kiss her. That more than anything made her settle down and stop second guessing everything.

Chapter 11

E mma watched Nancy and Fanny leave her office. Both agreed to join her recruitment campaign, which was the first step. She needed more women in the force, as police and community support officers. Thorndale had no women, which was inexcusable.

Although the current DI, Edmund Reeve, was such an ass that placing any woman there would be difficult.

"Night, ma'am," Dani said as she left. It was Wednesday. Emma had leftovers for dinner so she could get work done, relax, and still go to bed at a decent time.

Three a.m. came *ridiculously* early, after all. Her alarm went off and she cursed herself for signing up for the four a.m. slot.

"I'll learn to say no to Mrs. McCarthy," Emma vowed to herself as she slipped her feet into slippers. "Damn it, Em," she cursed as she grabbed her robe and headed downstairs. At least the coffee was brewing as she followed the smell into the kitchen.

"It's not enough to be present; you must be *present*," Mrs. McCarthy had told all the volunteers at their orientation meeting the week before Lent started. And reminded them when they agreed to continue on through the election of the new Pope.

"How is she going to know?" Emma wondered aloud as she dropped some toast into the toaster. "Like, the Lord is not going to rat on me to Mrs. McCarthy. I'm pretty sure." Emma sighed. But Mrs. McCarthy had put the fear of God in all of them, so here she was making sure she not only was alert and awake but a functioning human being for her hour slot at adoration.

"She must have been MI5 at some point," Emma decided as she got dressed. She would come back to get ready for work so she put on jeans and a comfortable sweater. Then to make sure she didn't fall asleep, she brought coffee. She'd risk Mrs. McCarthy's wrath with the coffee, but she'd never hear the end of it if she fell asleep. *Lesser of two evils*, she thought.

She arrived at St. Margaret and parked next to the other car in the lot, a man named Douglas. They exchanged pleasantries as she entered, and he grabbed his jacket.

A text half an hour in surprised her and she saw that the woman after her was running late. By the time she arrived and apologized profusely, it was closer to 5:30 when Emma got to her car. She pulled out and saw blue lights in the direction opposite of her flat, curious she turned to head that way.

She parked on the street far enough away she wouldn't bother the ambulance or cop car as she realized it was the same apartment complex with the domestic call prior. She pulled out the police jacket she carried with her and grabbed her radio and radioed dispatch to see what the call was.

"Neighbors called in a domestic. Same unit as previous call, ma'am."

She gripped her steering wheel because she didn't want to punch it but needed to do something with her hands. She was about to ask who was responding when she thought she recognized the back of Ollie's head heading into the unit. *He's not on shift. They all wear the same hat. There's no reason to think it's him.*

Rationality lost as she jumped out, throwing the police jacket on as she walked. She knew the danger was over if the ambulance was there...but the fact an ambulance was needed had her heart racing.

They'd have called you if any officer was hurt, Emma she reminded herself. It was the one part of her job she absolutely dreaded.

She approached the front of the ambulance facing the street, which hid most of what was happening from view. She quickened her footsteps and could finally see around the ambulance.

The scene was as horrible as she expected—the woman loaded up in the ambulance, the man in cuffs on the curb.

She turned the corner of the ambulance just as Oliver was carrying out a girl, maybe three years old, who was clutching a stuffed dog to her chest, eyes wide and watery.

Emma didn't want to interrupt. The scene was organized and the chaos had long passed. Her heart was just returning to normal and she forced herself to pay attention to everyone on the scene even if she wanted to check in on Oliver more than anything. There was PC Yasmin talking with a pair of community support officers after they deposited the man in the back of a squad car. The young woman officer—girl, who was Emma kidding—was still way too pale. Oliver was still holding the child, and Emma guessed he was waiting for child protective services.

First, she went to the officer that needed her. "PC Yasmin," Emma said as she approached, giving all three of them a nod. "Ma'am," Bakshi said, clearly just noticing she was there. "You read him his rights?" Emma asked. The last thing she wanted was for this case to get kicked out for a mistake on her officer's part. And the girl was young; the mistake would haunt her.

"Yes ma'am." Yasmin nodded. "Barnes witnessed it."

"How did he come to be here? His shift doesn't start for another ninety minutes," Emma said, looking at her watch.

"I texted him, ma'am. He and PC Halliwell both said to let them know if I got called here again while alone. Barnes insisted, as he lives five minutes away."

Emma nodded. "Take him down and finish your report. Good job."

"Yes, ma'am."

Emma saw the ambulance pulling out and stepped out of the way. Yasmin followed in her police car. She could finally find Oliver. And the breath she'd been holding finally was released seeing he was fine.

Just to be replaced as quickly with a different pain.

"And who is this cutie?" Emma asked the scared girl.

"This is Jenny," Oliver said as the girl clung to his neck tightly, her stuffed dog in a death grip, breaking Emma's heart. "CPS said it could be a bit before they're here, and I don't have a car."

"I'll give you a ride to the station," Emma said. "My car is down the street. Not far." When they reached it she opened the back door for him; since she didn't have a car seat, he would hold her for the couple of miles they had to go.

"Jenny does your dog have a name?" she heard him ask as they drove. The girl didn't answer any of Oliver's questions, at least not that Emma could hear, but a quick glance in the rearview mirror showed she snuggled tighter to Oliver, who kept talking to her. Maybe Jenny responded, but too quietly for Emma to hear.

Regardless it suddenly felt like she was leading Oliver on. She had come to terms with her own decision regarding children, but that was before she met Oliver and before she ever thought she would actually have an opportunity to be with someone.

Then she met him and she was thirty-six. And he was adorable in this horrible situation, handling it correctly. Right at the age she decided she would give up on *that* idea.

She waited with them until CPS arrived and they had an hour until shift began. "I have to change," Emma said, realizing she was still in jeans and a sweater. "I'm assuming you haven't eaten breakfast. Do you want to come to my place? I don't have time for a full English, but I do have things to fix for breakfast."

"Are you sure?"

"I wouldn't have offered if I wasn't." She nodded towards the door, and he followed her lead.

"Yasmin explained why you were there," Emma said.

"After seeing the size of that guy, I don't blame her for wanting backup."

"Why wasn't her partner working?" Emma asked.

"Called in sick. Flu is going around." Oliver sighed.

She could tell she surprised him by parking on the street out front. "It's faster," Emma pointed out. "How do you like your eggs?"

"Any way, I'm not picky." She opened the door, and he followed her through to the kitchen. She quickly made more coffee to brew before running upstairs to change.

Oliver watched her come downstairs and all exhaustion was gone. Back in her uniform—business slacks and blouse with her blazer on the back of a chair—she was professional, yet just as breathtaking as when she wore jeans and a sweater, or that incredibly soft dress he couldn't get out of his mind.

"Help yourself," Emma said as she handed him a cup. Sugar was already out in her little coffee station and she had grabbed the small carton of milk from the fridge with some eggs.

He leaned against the opposite counter. It looked out into the living area, but his attention was focused solely on Emma, who was currently whisking eggs in a bowl.

"Why were you up?" he asked. "Surely dispatch didn't call you."

"Adoration hour turned into Adoration hour and a half. When I left I saw the lights and put it together, although you being there was a surprise," she said.

She grabbed two plates while he heard the sausage frying. It came together quickly, which he knew it must, as they were on a deadline. She plated both of their breakfasts and brought them to the little table.

He found himself running his hand through her hair, his other hand wrapping around her waist as she turned and tucked herself against him. "I know we don't get a lot of domestic calls here. You were great," she whispered before placing a kiss at the pulse point in his neck.

"Thank you for this."

"Horrible way to start a morning. It's the least I could do."

"Hardly," Oliver promised and tilted her face up to capture a kiss. It was soft and gentle, like this little domestic moment, so opposite from how his morning had started.

He easily decided right then and there he wanted to spend every morning starting like this.

"You even smell good." He smiled before reluctantly letting go of her to pull out her chair for her. The slightest blush on her cheeks made him grin as he took his own seat.

"Tell me something about your job today," he said.

She swallowed as she thought. "Well, Nancy and Fanny both agreed to be part of the recruitment campaign I have planned. I have interns working on some things and I'll figure out how to fit them in."

"Nancy looks up to you like you're Wonder Woman. Pretty sure if you asked for a kidney, she'd give you one," Oliver teased.

"Come on." Emma laughed as she stood and took their plates to the sink to deal with later. "I'll drop you off, yeah?"

"I could get used to this if you're not careful, Emma St. George."

I could get used to this.

Ollie's voice percolated in her brain all day. Between the lack of sleep, fear over Oliver, and now these thoughts, she was pretty useless at work.

"Do you want to talk about it?" Dani asked.

"Nothing to talk about, Sergeant, unless it is the upcoming sergeant exams. Did PC Halliwell sign up?"

"Yes'm. She is the only one in your district to this time around," Dani said.

Emma studied the older woman. "I am too tired to try to figure out if you are hinting at something."

"I'm not. But there will be others who do, who question. At least for awhile."

"There's nothing to question. Or there won't be," Emma sighed. "Now I have phone calls to make and you have final preparations for the party to plan," she said, dismissing the woman.

"Pool hall has confirmed, and there are approximately twelve off-duty officers across all five station houses who said they would attend. I'll send a reminder email," Dani said as she stood to leave. "For what it's worth, bringing them all together to socialize is a great idea."

Emma just nodded, not caring. She felt confident that her idea was good and would be successful, even if HQ didn't give her a budget to work with. They were all small jurisdictions, and while the officers all technically knew of each other, they never had a reason to become better acquainted outside of the occasional call for assistance.

At the moment, though, everything made her feel prickly. Having others, as Dani insinuated, pick and poke at her relationship with Oliver made her feel like a bug being inspected under a microscope.

Lack of sleep, scary morning, nothing more, she told herself. Because she hadn't worried about it. She felt comfortable around Oliver in a way she didn't think she would, between his age and her lack of relationships. But there were definitely some major roadblocks and now that she saw them she couldn't unsee them.

She didn't care about what others thought, but she did care if she cheated him of something he wanted later in life. It would break her heart if he came to resent her, she realized.

Chapter 12

Oliver found her on the way out of door. "I figure you are too tired to cook after this day, want to grab something?"

"Actually, I was thinking we should talk. She looked around and wished she could banish all people from the village. She nodded down the alley where the back of her office lined up against a forest with a walking trail. A few feet in would give them some semblance of privacy at least.

"Oliver." Emma took a breath. "It's been fun."

"No," he interrupted. "Don't cheapen this, us. 'It's been fun'? What, are we in high school?"

"No. But I haven't exactly done this before, so I don't know how one goes about ending something before it gets too big. Be honest, Ollie. There's a reason we haven't done the paperwork," she said. "Because yes, this has been fun. More than fun. So much more than fun," she admitted. "But have you really thought about it? Not the seniority stuff, but everything else? I'm thirty-six. I'm always going to be older. God, I *feel* old thinking about my twenties. You're not there yet." There was so much he still didn't realize was ahead of him.

"You're not that old or cynical," he countered. "Don't put yourself down, Em."

She heard the temper in his voice, so different from his affable nature. "I am being practical. I don't want to have kids, not at my age. By the time I get pregnant I'll be having a 'geriatric' pregnancy, and I don't want to go through that. I don't want to be retired at their graduation from high school. The world is going to hell, and I can't see bringing new life into it with everything going on, with kids already in deplorable conditions." She shook her head. "That's something I have to deal with, have had to wrestle with, and I have. I've accepted that I focused on my career first and that I'm going against my church's teachings. I've mourned because it was a real loss to me but have come to accept my decision. You haven't thought about that part of things, though," she guessed. "You are at the beginning of everything and can do so many things, in terms of family and career. My rank is important, but there are other things, too. We're at different parts of our lives and want different things."

"Emma."

"Oliver, I know you haven't thought about it. We haven't talked about it."

"Your career was the most important thing; always has been. That is clear. Why bother talking about it? Is this you running away from us because I'll hold you back?"

Her jaw dropped open. "What? I can handle my career just fine, thank you very much. If you're hung up on that, that's on you. Which I think proves my point that we're at two very different points in our lives."

"Emma." He reached out, desperate to hold her, but she stepped back.

"Ollie. Listen. I'm so grateful you asked for those four dates and that we had all the rest." She smiled and had to force herself not to cry. Not here, not now. "Two different stages of life."

"Bullshit. It's not *that* big of an age difference."

"It's not the years, it's the end goal." She could feel the burn of unshed tears and knew the avalanche was coming soon. The last thing she needed was to cry in public, cry in front of him. "Thankfully I leave for that working vacation soon, and by the time I get back it will be nothing but fun memories. Ravenswick will move on to some other gossip."

"Emma."

"You can't say you have honestly thought about it, so what is the point in arguing, Oliver?"

"I didn't think you were the type to give up without a fight."

"Maybe I'm tired of fighting, of everything always being a fight." What she wanted to say was she didn't know how to fight this, fight for this, because if she let it, it had the potential to become so much more important than anything else in her life.

The short commute to her flat felt like forever. She refused to cry since she was driving, but she could feel it coming on, her breath shaky. Finally, she reached her road.

Anne sat outside her door. Emma didn't know why, but she was so thankful her best friend was there. When Anne saw Emma walk through the gate, she raised the bottle of wine in her hand. Once inside, she poured glasses for both of them and, knowing Emma's flat as well as her own, took out the emergency frozen pizza to pop in the oven.

"What happened? Dani called me directly and said she thought something might be going on with you and Oliver, and that I should check on you."

"What?" Emma asked in shock, sinking onto her couch.

"What happened, love? Because I could tell on your face when you parked that something happened."

"It can't work out, Anne," Emma insisted and suddenly the floodgates opened. She repeated everything she told Oliver. Since it was Anne she went into her fears, that one day he would resent her for her decisions.

She didn't even want to eat but had her portion of the pizza solely so Anne wouldn't nag her.

"I could just see him in ten years looking at me in resentment. Looking at old-lady me and thinking this—the two of us— isn't enough." Emma downed the last of her wine.

"I'm in the 'men are idiots' camp right now, so I'm not defending any of them. I am sorry you're hurting, though," Anne wrapped an arm around her shoulders where they sat on the couch together.

Looking at the time she helped Emma to her feet. "We can just be two old ladies together," Anne promised as she prompted Emma up the stairs so she could change out of her work clothes. "I'd prefer a dog to a cat, but open to negotiation in that."

"A pair of confirmed Austen Saint bachelorettes," Emma agreed. "Big dogs. Oh, my cousins know someone who raises Irish Wolfhounds."

"Go shower. I'll clean up downstairs," Anne said. "You've been up since God knows when," she realized aloud, looking at the time.

Emma dragged herself to her bathroom and went through the motions. She was bone-weary. It was hardly the first time she'd dragged herself through her routine, just to plop down on her bed and pass out for however many hours she had. It was the first time she was doing it while devastated over a man.

She decided she deserved a good wallow and pulled her plush robe on after her quick shower. Then practically face-planted into her pillow.

Anne came and sat on her bed, lying down when Emma patted it. It was suddenly like when they were in high school having sleepovers and the fact Emma was back in Ravenswick hit her. Her life was full circle.

"Get some sleep," Anne said. "It hurts less in the morning."

"I feel like that's a lie, but I'm going to hold you to that. It was the little girl," Emma said, suddenly confusing Anne. "It was hardly my first domestic case, and all my officers did their jobs well. It just...it was a kick in the gut to see him holding this beautiful little child. She was so scared, so confused, and latched on to Oliver as her port in the storm. He'd be a great dad. And I mourned this part of my life, Anne. I did. But it just felt like being hit by a two-by-four."

"You mourned but never had anyone. It was probably like losing it all over again."

Tears ran down Emma's cheeks because Anne understood. "Am I wrong? That I won't change my mind?"

"I can't tell you what to do, or what to feel. You know my thoughts on it, how could I ever judge you? Get some sleep."

Too exhausted to say anything more, Emma finally slipped into a deep sleep.

Chapter 13

Emma opened the door to the pool hall and could hear the joking and laughter before she could see anyone. Hopefully that was a good sign. Once she turned the corner and entered the hall, she could see the assorted officers: some playing darts, some sitting at various tables gabbing. The two DIs present were grabbing a drink at the bar.

"Chief." Neville noticed her and waved her over to the bar.

"Inspectors," she greeted them and waved away the bartender. "This is a good turnout."

"Glad you approve," Edmund muttered, and Emma ignored him. He had always been the most difficult officer in her precinct and had resented her presence since she arrived.

"I promised to be the drink deliverer," Neville said as the tray was finally loaded up and he took it over to a table with his DS and a couple other officers.

"How are things in Thorndale, Inspector?" Emma asked Edmund and pointed to a bottle of water. The bartender grabbed one for her.

"Grand, as you know."

"You were never one to mince words, I'll give you that," Emma drawled as she twisted off the cap.

Oliver caught her eye and she missed the easiness between them. At least now it was clear how to behave when in a room together—separate individuals, and she outranked him. Clear distinctions, clear boundaries.

Anne had lied. It hadn't gotten easier in the morning, but Emma had too much work to wallow.

She missed him.

Edmund caught her look and smirked. "I can't help but wonder if there should be an investigation. I keep going back and forth over that in my mind."

Distracted, Emma asked, "What investigation?" There were no big potential cases pending in his precinct; she had no idea what he was referring to.

"Into your relationship with the Barnes boy."

That caught her attention, and she took one more drink of her water before reclosing the lid. She set it down carefully and turned to give Edmund her full attention.

He said, "If the roles were reversed someone would demand an investigation." His smirk made her feel slimy and she wanted to smack it off of him but knew that was the reaction he was going for. Instead she relaxed her hands letting the tension go out of her body.

Then she smiled—not smirk, no sarcasm. A smile like a mother gives her misbehaving child. "Really? Do it."

The shock on his face was hilarious. He clearly expected her to plead or deny or defend.

"You'll find this: nothing," she said. "First, there is no relationship to investigate. Even if there were, however, it wouldn't matter. In fact..."

Emma stood, feeling the need to be her whole height. "I order you to do it regardless, as there may be questions of our past interactions. This will help clear any future concerns. I will let my office know to expect phone calls to arrange interviews in the morning. A bit speedy, but you should know that I will be out of the country by the end of the week. Working vacation pre-approved months ago. Now..." She grabbed her water and her purse.

"One last question, Inspector. Would you have confidently made that declaration if your superior officer in question was a man? We'll speak soon," she promised. She walked back out of the hall and out to her car.

The worst part was she wanted Oliver. She wanted to talk to him, vent to him, be held by him, and that wasn't going to happen.

She hit the button on her screen to call her sister. "Can you come by?"

"Of course. You okay?"

"No."

It didn't take a genius to know something happened between Emma and the DI from Thorndale. Oliver noticed several officers exchanging glances. "Come on," Nancy said, standing and pulling his arm. He had no idea what she was planning, but if it got him out of this building, so be it.

"For what it's worth, I think most everyone in there would punch him in the face," Nancy whispered to him as they headed out.

He didn't know what to say to that. Great; everyone recognized the guy was a twat? *Hooray*, he thought sarcastically.

"Look, you and I left together, so there'll be no wagging tongues," Nancy said. "Go after her. I'll head home. No one has to know—"

"Bloody hell," Oliver interrupted her and nodded behind Nancy. She turned as he said, "Seriously, what are the odds?"

Weeks of searching and tonight was the night they finally caught a sighting of their thief. Taking a lazy walk about town as if he had no cares in the world. "Hang on," Nancy said and reached for her phone and texted someone. "Someone from Brackenmoor is coming out, it's their jurisdiction."

A moment later their DS, Fanny Fletcher, came out with a woman Oliver knew was a constable from the local station, but her name escaped him. "That's him. The man in the tapes with the Monstrance from St. Margaret's," Oliver said as he pointed at the individual in question, and the three constables took off.

About the only thing going Oliver's way that night was the fact the guy didn't run off, so Oliver was spared a nighttime chase in a village he barely knew the layout of.

"Do you want to question him here?" the local PC asked.

Fanny rejoined them. "I've sorted it; he'll come down with us. Keep me in the loop, Barnes," Fanny ordered before heading back inside.

"Of all the nights to finally get the son of a…" Oliver slammed the door shut after they secured the guy in the backseat of their cruiser.

He saw Nancy look over to the pool hall. "What?"

"The DS specifically said for you to keep her in the loop."

"What, you want to go back to the party?"

She angled so they were both facing down the street, so the perp in the back couldn't see what they said. If anyone else came out of the pool hall, they wouldn't immediately hear them, either.

"I'm curious—don't get me wrong. That inspector Reeve does *not* seem popular, even before whatever he said to upset the chief super. No, my point was the DS could have come down with me, but she wanted you to work. Which tells me she doesn't think you should go after Emma."

"The universe is against me tonight."

"Or it's not."

He was ready to throttle his partner. Nancy laughed, seeing his frustrated face. "I don't know everything you fought about.

I don't need to. But having had my share of fights, let me ask you this: have you heard what she said? Because if you are still just reacting to the hurt of breaking up and not listening, that won't get you far."

"I still hate you and the universe at the moment," Oliver grumbled as he opened the driver door. But her words percolated as he went through the process of booking the man and the interrogation, although he really was just a seat filler during the interview.

"For what it's worth," Oliver told Nancy when they were finally done and heading out, "you'll make a great sergeant."

"I know." Nancy smiled. "For the record, you would too. Look around; it's Ravenswick, not London. You'd have plenty to do on this side of the desk, too." With a wave, she walked out the main entrance.

Leaving him with even more to think about. All the thinking, though, was giving way to a plan.

Chapter 14

Emma heard the knock on the back door and had no idea who it could be. It was a Saturday and she felt run down. Her vacation at the end of the week couldn't come soon enough. The idea of seeing Oliver around the village for the next five days threatened to make her cry. Again.

"What the hell?" Emma wondered aloud upon opening the door to Oliver.

"Can I come in? Otherwise I'm sure whichever of the Austen Saints are home will hear us."

"There's nothing to hear," Emma pointed out, but stepped aside.

"There's lots," Oliver promised. "First, we made an arrest in the theft at St. Margaret's. We're working on getting the monstrance back from whom it was sold to."

"Mrs. McCarthy will get off my back, then."

"I feel like it's safe to assume Charlie told her by now."

Oliver smiled and she wanted to smack him for coming into her home while being charming and gorgeous, and kiss him because he was charming and gorgeous, and then smack him again for the rollercoaster of emotions.

"I don't know what the DI said to you the other night. I know it had to be awful, and I wanted nothing more than to punch his lights out. I didn't, obviously, but I wanted you to know that it was because I knew you had handled the situation. I still want to punch him," Oliver grumbled.

"And that would prove both of us right at the same time." Emma rolled her eyes as she leaned against the cupboard in the kitchen, facing Oliver who was leaning against the table. "So you caught the thief and refrained from punching a superior officer. A good day for the Ravenswick police constabulary, then."

"I've thought about what you said. All of what you said. And what you didn't say."

"What didn't I say?"

"I'll get to that. First, papers," Oliver announced and pulled out a set of folded papers and handed them to her. "I've filled out and signed them. You're turn."

"For what? Holy hell, Oliver." Emma looked up sharply from reading the first page, seeing it was the paperwork to declare interoffice dating. "What part of my conversation wasn't clear? I'm usually effective in my communication."

"As I said, I heard what you said, Emma. And I thought about it. I can't do anything about the age difference, I would catch up to you in a heartbeat if I could. I didn't think about having a family before. Part of me just assumed it would happen because that's what couples do. If it happens it happens. What I do know is this potential future family isn't more important than you, Em."

He slowly reached out to take her free hand. "Kids or not, to me what is important is waking up knowing my day begins and ends with you. And because it's Ravenswick that also means pretty good odds of seeing you in the middle of the day, too." He smirked, seeing he teased a reluctant smile out of her.

"Oliver. I saw the way you were with that girl, Jenny, and you were amazing in the worst possible situation. You would be an amazing dad, if you want that. It's a big thing and I don't want you to regret losing something later."

"Not saying it isn't," he promised. "I am saying that you are even more important. Whatever the future looks like, I want you there in the center of it with me. I want it to be you and me. That is enough for me, Emma. That is more than I ever imagined when I was running into door frames or nearly breaking DS Fletcher's rib in a rugby tackle. Please don't ask for details."

"Oliver." She sighed, then narrowed her eyes as he took her hand, still clasped in his, and brought it up to kiss her knuckles.

"Two more things. I heard what you didn't say."

"That is quite the talent."

"I'm a talented guy." Oliver smiled and she was definitely, absolutely a goner. She wasn't even trying to create any kind of distance between them. She didn't get to where she was by being a pushover and here she was just lapping up everything Oliver was saying.

"You said this was your first real relationship. Hang on," he said as she tried to jerk her hand away. She didn't regret telling him, at least not in the moment, but it did make her feel queasy with shame. Both because it was true, and because she had been so open about it.

"Hey," Oliver said, stepping forward to close the distance between them. "This is what I thought I saw the other day. Maybe I didn't, but it has to be a factor. Don't run from me, Emma."

"Why? Just why." She sighed. "You can skip all this awkwardness on my part. Do you know how embarrassing it is to feel completely lost? I've never *not* known what to do and here I am just flying by the seat of my pants, I feel like, waiting for everyone to notice."

"Speaking for myself, what does it matter? You were waiting on me. Sorry you had to wait so long."

Emma laughed and he used it as an opportunity to wrap his arms gently around her waist. "You said two things," she reminded him.

"Hmm. I signed up for the sergeant exams," he said, and her jaw dropped.

"What the hell? Like *what the bloody hell*?"

"I can't do anything about our ages. I can do something about my rank. I don't promise to do more," he added quickly. "But if I pass, I can at least not be a lowly PC."

"You'll pass, but no." Emma shook her head. "You don't want to, and I don't want to make you feel like you are changing for me."

"I'm changing my rank, not *me*," he said. "It took me a minute to realize that. I can imagine what your superiors and everyone else will think. I worried it was also what you thought—that I'd be keeping you down by staying as a PC."

"I told you; the only rank I care about is my own. I don't need you to do this."

"I do. I don't know if I can keep moving up, but I need to do this," he insisted. "Now will you kiss me and put me out of my misery?"

Emma laughed and twisted around away from him, making him huff in frustration. She didn't break away from his arms, though; she grabbed a pen on the counter and set the papers down, flipping to the back page to add her signature next to his.

"There. Happy?" Emma drawled as she turned to face him again. Her tone might have been sarcastic, but her smile was pure delight.

"*Ecstatic* doesn't quite cover it," Oliver promised, smiling. One hand came up to thread through her hair as he captured her lips in a kiss.

About the author

Christina Clare is a Catholic convert, cat mom (dog aunt!), environmentalist, and nerd. Her alter ego is a college professor where she has published on a variety of things, including Pope Francis.

When not working or writing, you will probably find her reading or binge watching British murder mysteries. Or taking care of her cats now that she inherited more. Follow along on instagram or facebook (@Christina Clare, author), or her newsletter where you'll be the first to know about the next book.